Something *

Christop   ....u

In Memory of Barbara.

A wonderful loving Sister.

Without her help this book would
have remained just words on pieces
of paper.

Something About Nothing
by
Christopher Reed

Keeping a secret

It was a warm, sunny, August morning. There was nothing unusual about this particular day.

Rebecca reached deep into the rock pool as Martin held her hand for safety, while Anna watched with excitement.

It was nothing for the three of them to spend all day trying to recover things that had been washed up by the previous evening's tide.

Having struggled to lift what they all were hoping to be something of interest, their faces said it all, as they peered into yet another old, rusty can.

It seems so unfair that people throw rubbish into our ocean. This was what they had grown to refer to, the strip of coastline they had all known since a very early age. "Our bit of ocean. How can they do this?" Anna said with harshness in her voice, clearly showing her displeasure.

"Come on," said Martin "let's go and look in the other pools. We can surely find something. It was very stormy last night and we've never failed to find something after a storm."

As they walked along the rocky coastline they all stopped suddenly as something very strange caught their eyes. As they looked up the cliff face, they could all see very clearly a well trodden path. The path had become overgrown with brambles and shrubs for many years and, unless someone had thought about clearing the rock face, it would have stayed hidden for many more.

"What do you think caused this to happen?" Rebecca said, with a puzzled look on her face.

"It may have been done by the high winds and rain we had last night," said Martin.

Those plants had hung onto the cliff face for as long as they could and last night their roots just pulled away from the rocks.

"Come on!" said Martin "let's take a look!" As they reached the bottom of the cliff it was clear they would not be able to reach the path from the beach. "Hang on," said Martin. "If we all go up to the top of the cliff we may be able to reach the path from there." Once on the path it was Martin who led the way. "Come on!"

With great excitement Martin ran ahead of the girls, who were both finding it difficult to keep up. Brambles and bushes blocked the path. This slowed Martin down and gave the girls a chance to catch up. "We'll need to clear a path," he said, shouting back to the girls. They watched as he pushed his way through the tangled mess. Now they were almost at the end of the path, they could clearly see an entrance to a tunnel.

"What do we do now?" said Anna, sounding rather bothered about the situation.

"Shouldn't we tell someone first?"

Martin hadn't heard any of this as he was busy clearing the entrance.

"Come on," said Martin. He was standing in the entrance to the tunnel and would have gone without the girls if they didn't keep up.

They had only gone in a little way when it began to get too dark to see anything. All of them held hands with a grip that was almost unbearable. "Stop!" cried Rebecca. "This is silly. We could fall or something and no one knows we are here!"

"Don't be a baby!" said Martin. "If you're too scared, I can go on my own."

"No. Stop!" shouted Rebecca. "This is stupid!" The other two heard the anger in her voice. "Martin you are crazy to even think of going in there on your own. Or is this yet another of your adventures?" she continued. "Anyway, it is far too dangerous even if YOU can't see it?"

Martin stopped in his tracks, not wanting the girls to know he was pleased to have an excuse to go back to the daylight. As he turned he felt something under his foot. He was not about to stay and find out what it was, so, quickly, he grabbed the girls' hands and made a quick dash out of the tunnel entry and into the safety of daylight. "What do we do now?" said Anna. "If our parents find out about this, I'm sure they will stop us coming down here again."

"Hang on" said Martin. Martin was forever saying 'hang on'. He had become well known for it to the point where anyone who knew him, would refer to him as 'Hang on Harris' his surname being Harris. Still, he never meant anything by it and would often use it without even realising that he had said it.

"Hang on," he said. "Let's not rush home and tell anyone anything about this. I think this should be our secret for now. Let's just keep it to ourselves until we've had a chance to think about what we should do."

On the way back home they discussed what they had found and what they might find.

Stories of hidden treasure were discussed, along with lost cities and strange worlds.

It was hard to sleep, for all of them, that night as thoughts rushed through their heads.

The next day was as bright and windy as the previous day had been. As Martin dressed all he could think about was how quickly he could eat his breakfast, that he knew his mother was sure to insist he had, and would the girls be ready?

As he sat eating a rather soggy piece of toast, the doorbell rang. This made him jump so much that the toast he was eating fell into his now cold cup of tea. Looking down at the bits of toast floating in his cup, he picked it up and in one gulp it was gone! Tea and toast in one go.

That's breakfast out of the way, now don't rush too quickly, he told himself. Mum will think there's something up.

"Martin, darling! It's Rebecca and Anna," his mother called. He hated it when is mum called him darling, especially in front of friends. 'Darling' seemed so silly. It was one of those words they used in really old films.

It wasn't long before the three of them were sat at the top of the cliff looking down onto the path. "Do you think anyone else has seen the path?" asked Anna. "Let's hope not," whispered Rebecca, just in case anyone was listening to them talking.

"Look," said Martin. "It's too late for that now. We should have covered the path before we left last night, but we all left in rather a hurry. If you hadn't been so scared we wouldn't have run away like we did," Martin pointed his accusing finger at the girls.

"Us! Scared! It was you pulling us," said Rebecca. "My hand still hurts because you squeezed it so tight."

"Sorry," said Martin, feeling rather guilty that he was blaming the girls, but he still felt it was as much them as him, who wanted to get back in the daylight and away from this strange place.

They hadn't been there that long when they noticed someone coming along the beach. "That's it now," said Anna "He's bound to see the path if he looks this way."

"Not if we stop him," said Martin.

"Come on, quick, down to the beach." They all ran as fast as they could, stumbling over loose tufts of grass and rocks. As they ran along the sand they met Mr Richardson. He often walked his dog along this part of the beach before going to work.

"Morning," called Martin.

"A fine good morning to you," came the reply.

"Where's your dog?"

"He's around here somewhere. You know what dogs are like. He's probably picked up the scent of a rabbit or something." Martin whistled trying to act as normal as he could. He'd now reached the water's edge which meant that Mr Richardson would be looking out to sea.

If he could only keep his attention away from the cliff and looking out to sea that would stop him looking back at the cliff and seeing the path. "What's that in the water?" said Martin, "it's not your dog is it Mr Richardson?"

"Where? I can't see anything."

"Yes, there he is way out in the water." Mr Richardson strained his eyes through his glasses.

Removing them quickly he gave them a wipe with a not so clean hanky, replacing them firmly on his nose.

"Nope," he said "I can't see anything. Your eyes must be much better than mine or you're seeing things."

"There he is! There's your dog out there, look he's got to be five hundred metres at least from the beach" cried Rebecca, who could see clearly what Martin was trying to do.

"Nope, still can't see him," said Mr Richardson, now looking very concerned about his best friend and companion's safety. By this time they had walked past the bottom of the exposed cliff and were all relieved when this large, rather shaggy dog came bounding down the beach.

Mr Richardson laughed with relief and hugged the dog as it licked his face. "Good fella," he said "where have you been?"

"After the rabbits I expect," said Anna. "You don't think he could catch one do you Mr Richardson?" she asked feeling rather sorry for the poor rabbits.

"No, it's only in his dreams that he catches them, he's got a job to keep up with me these days. Well, home boy, then it's work for me," he said as he waved goodbye to the three children who had scared him only minutes before. "So long and have a nice day."

The children didn't hear him as he left. They were already making their way back to the bottom of the cliff. "Come on," said Martin "let's see if we can't hide the path."

The morning flew by as they worked to cover the path, which, by 11 o'clock was well hidden from view and all of them felt rather hungry. "Are we going home for something to eat, I'm starving," cried Martin from further up the path, "or do you want to take a look inside before we go home?"

"No! Not yet," answered Rebecca. "It was far too dark to see anything inside last time we went in. We need to get a torch or something." Martin was mad with himself. Why hadn't he thought of that?

"Good idea!" he said. "Let's go home and get some torches and we can grab something to eat at the same time."

As they were about to leave something sprung into Martin's head. "Hang on!" he called to the girls as he began making his way back to the tunnel entrance. It wasn't long before he was back and on the path with the girls. "Do you think we've covered the path enough?"

"Yes," said Anna who was feeling very hungry now and didn't care who could see the path.

Food was the only thing on her mind. They didn't call her hungry Anna for nothing!

No time for joking!

As soon as they had had something to eat and found torches they met at Anna's house.

Anna's house was the closest to the beach and was the best place to meet. "I've brought some wool," said Rebecca. "I thought we could use it in the tunnel to find our way back to the entrance."

"Come on, let's get going, it'll be dark before we get there." Anna was trying to understand what that meant as they were going to be in the dark anyway. Still, boys say funny things anyway, she thought to herself and smiled.

As they went down to the path Martin was giving out orders and seemed very impatient. "What's got into you?" Anna pulled on Martin's arm. "Don't you want us now?"

"Sure I do! But you know when we were leaving earlier? Well, I went just inside the mouth of the tunnel and as I turned to come out I felt something under my foot."

He held out his hands and there, cupped in them, was a shoe. It wasn't a shoe like you would see today. It was very simply made from leather and cord. It had no sole. It was more like a slipper than a shoe.

"Wonder where that came from?" Rebecca asked with renewed interest.

"I don't know but I think it's very old. Look at how the bottom is very worn and thin," said Martin.

"So, is that why you are in such a rush? You want to find the other shoe so you can try them on?" Anna began, laughing to herself.

"No, I want to put it back where I found it. It might be special or something," replied Martin. It was with more than just a little fear, that they all entered the tunnel.

Rebecca had fastened the end of the wool firmly to a rock just at the tunnel entrance and was feeding the wool out very slowly so as not to break it.

Martin was at the front and was being held back by Anna who had a very firm grip on the belt of his trousers.

Martin led the way slowly as there were many bits of rock on the floor of the tunnel which made it hard to walk. "Come on," he called but Anna was only going to go at her pace. She was in no hurry to go deeper into the damp, dark tunnel, which could contain who knows what?

"Come on," he called again. "Don't be scared, there's nothing in here. Listen."

They all stopped and listened. The only sounds they could hear were sounds of water dripping and echoing around the tunnel.

They continued walking until they reached the end of the passage. They were now standing in a large cavern and at the far end they found a very large shaft.

Martin estimated it to be twenty metres wide and at least forty metres deep. Just like boys thought Anna again.

They could see the bottom with the light of her torch so it could not be more than twenty metres deep. "What shall we do now?" asked Rebecca.

"I know," said Martin "let's get Anna to climb down."

"I'm not going down there!" she said in a quick response.

"Just joking," said Martin. How to get down and who would climb down, into the deep dark hole? "I'll go" said Martin smiling back at Anna.

They all looked down the shaft and could see a small steel ladder hanging down the one side. Martin lowered himself over the edge very slowly.

As he climbed onto the ladder all he could think about was how far did it go? In his normal way he had jumped in feet first, or, on this occasion, over rather than in.

How could he be so stupid?! Well it was too late now he was over the hardest part of finding the ladder in the dark with two girls yelling, "Be careful! And don't fall!"

Slowly he worked his way down the ladder. Rebecca and Anna looked on and still gave advice from the lip of the shaft. It seemed as though their friend had been descending for a long time when, suddenly, the torch that Martin had tied to his waist went out. Rebecca said nothing as she felt Anna's grip tighten on her arm.

"What do we do now?" whispered Anna.

"I don't know," Rebecca replied. They both shone their torches down into the darkness.

"Shall I go and get help?" said Anna. "I'll run as fast as I can to Mr Walter's house, it's only a short distance from here."

"Martin!" called Rebecca. "Martin!" she called again. There was no reply and it was hard to fight back tears as she continued to call his name.

"Don't cry, Rebecca," said Anna squeezing her arm tighter. "His torch may have run out."

"I don't think so," said Rebecca "or he would have answered."

"We better both go and get someone and tell them what has happened." Rebecca called down into the shaft once again. "Martin, if you can hear us, we are going to get help, we won't be long!"

They both stood up and turned to leave. "Where do you think you are going?" It was the sound of an all too familiar voice.

"Martin!" they both cried out.

There, only a short distance away, stood Martin. "But how did you get here?" asked Anna.

"Well, as I was going down the ladder I hadn't gone far when I found an entrance to a small passage. I simply stepped into the entrance and followed the passage which led to some steps, which brought me back to the top of the shaft."

"Look," he said "the entrance is just over there." He shone his torch and showed them where the entrance to the stairway was.

"I think you should have told us what you were going to do before you disappeared," said Rebecca.

"You could have been hurt or anything," said Anna. Rebecca was about to join in again when Martin burst out laughing.

"What's so funny?" said Rebecca.

"You," he said. "You look like a couple of panda's." Where they had been rubbing their tear filled eyes large white patches had been left around them.

"I don't think it's funny," said Rebecca.

Martin cut in "don't go on I'm okay and you're not hurt. I'm sorry I didn't tell you and I can see it was a very stupid thing to do. Look, we have to get on or our batteries will run out and then we will be stuck."

Martin led the way down the stone steps and out onto the ledge. He found getting onto the ladder much easier than before. "Let's see what's at the bottom this time," he said as he made his way down the ladder.

Reaching the bottom rung, he found himself some distance from the floor. "What are you doing?" said Anna.

"I'm at the bottom of the ladder," came the reply.

As Martin shone his torch down between his feet onto the floor below, he wasn't sure how far it was. This was partly due to the fact that his torch was now growing dimmer by the minute.

It looked only a short distance. "Well I've come this far and it doesn't look too high," here goes! he thought to himself, and then jumped down from the ladder. Martin's feet hit the floor a lot harder than he had expected.

Looking up, panic quickly ran through his body. The bottom of the ladder was at least three metres from the floor. Martin, being only one and half metres tall, realised that unless he could jump like a well trained high jumper, he was not going to be able to reach the ladder.

He called up to the girls. "I think I may need some help. The ladder is much further from the floor than I thought and I don't think I can reach it."

"That's great!" called Rebecca. "What do we do now?"

"Go and get help," said Anna, who was getting a bit fed up with it all. Boys do some silly things she thought again.

"Hang on!" came the call from below. It all seemed very quiet and the dim light had now disappeared again.

"Where are you now?" called Rebecca. There was no reply. "Martin!" she called again. "Martin where are you?" There was still no reply from the darkness.

"What can he be doing?" Anna called into the darkness below.

"I don't know," said Rebecca. "Better look behind us in case he jumps out of nowhere and gives us both a fright."

It wasn't long before the dim light returned. "You're back then!" Anna called sounding rather annoyed.

"Won't be long," came the reply.

The light disappeared again. When Martin returned he called up to the girls "I'm okay, I'll be with you in just a few minutes."

It wasn't long before Martin had reached the girls who both still looked rather funny with their white eyes. "How did you get back onto the ladder?" they both asked.

"Well, you'll never believe what's down there."

"What? What?" Anna pleaded.

"Well, there's a great cavern. It's more like a hall and it's got lots of tables and chairs. It's all set out like some kind of meeting place. It's all very old and most of the chairs and tables are broken. There must be at least a hundred tables and many more chairs. All I had to do was find an unbroken table and chair to stand on to reach the ladder," said Martin. "Once I did that it was easy getting back up here."

"You're very clever," said Anna. Martin finally felt he had done something right.

"Look," he said "let's get out of here now, my torch has just about had it, and I think we had better find somewhere for you both to wash your faces or we will have some very difficult questions to answer."

They followed the wool back to the entrance. They all set about replacing branches and twigs across the path, ensuring the path they had found was well hidden, before heading down to the beach to wash and clean themselves before returning home.

"What's next?" said Rebecca.

"I've been thinking about that," said Martin and suggested that they should all meet later to discuss what should be done. "I'll come round to your house Rebecca," he said. "Can you come around?" he asked Anna.

"Can't see why not," she said. "We're always visiting each other so no one will object as long as I'm not too late."

"Seven o'clock, Rebecca's house," said Martin and they all nodded in agreement.

Martin was the first to arrive at Rebecca's home. Standing on the front porch, he rang the doorbell. The door opened and there stood Mr Crabtree. "Good evening to you, Martin."

"Come on in, Rebecca's here somewhere?" "Rebecca", called her father. "Martins here."

Rebecca came running into the hall. "No Anna?"

"Haven't seen her," replied Martin. "Let's go out and wait on the front porch," said Rebecca. They both rushed to the front door and were relieved to get outside where they could talk about their plans. Just as they had both started talking of the day's events Anna arrived. "Deciding what to do without me!?" she said rather bluntly.

"No," said Martin, "we just got outside the house as you arrived."

"What's wrong Anna?" said Rebecca.

"Nothing, it's just that you two seem to be deciding everything without me. Maybe I should go so you can make your own plans without me."

"Don't be silly," said Martin. "This is our secret. Yours, Rebecca's and mine. Come on tell us what do you think we should do?"

"Well," said Anna "I think we should ..."

Once Anna got started it seemed there was no stopping her. She had lots of ideas and as the others listened they were both surprised. "Well!" exclaimed Martin. "Did you have any time for tea? You must have spent the last hour thinking about what to do next." Anna laughed! "Don't be silly, I can eat and think at the same time."

Once the discussions had finished they'd all agreed that before they did anything else they would see if they could find anything out about the long lost tunnel and shoe they had found. To do this they all agreed to meet the next day when they would visit the local library and museum in town. Anna left the meeting feeling very pleased with herself. She, for once, was the one being listened to instead of just nodding in agreement as the others decided what they would do. Anna had always felt a little left out, and had accepted it, as she was younger than the others, who were at least two years older.

Discovery

The following morning they had all caught the 8:30 bus into town so they would be at the library when it opened at 9:00. Once inside they went straight to the reference section and hunted through the books.

They had been looking for more than an hour when they were interrupted. "What is it you're looking for?" asked the librarian in a voice that sent a chill running down their spines.

"Can I help?" she said peering over the top of her glasses. They all said nothing at first.

Rebecca was the first to answer. "We're looking for books about this area. We are particularly interested in the coast and cliffs. Has anyone written about them?"

"I don't know," said the librarian, "I'll take a look," and she left them to go back to her desk.

Martin gave Rebecca a prod in the back. "What are you doing?" You might as well tell her everything!"

"What was I going to say?" said Rebecca.

"I don't know, but the fewer people we tell about our secret the better," muttered Martin.

"I didn't say anything about the tunnel or shoe did I?" said Rebecca.

"No, but if we tell her too much she may ask some difficult questions," said Martin.

As they finished arguing the librarian returned. "Here you are. These are the books we currently have on this area. They may include something about the coast and cliffs." She handed them a computer printout which had three books on it.

"You may find out something at the local museum," she said and left them to return to her desk.

"Come on!" said Martin. "Let's get these books and go to the museum. Seems like your idea to go to the museum was a good one, Anna!"

"Who would have thought it? You being so clever!" said Rebecca.

Anna now felt needed, not just a hanger on. They collected the books and left the library to take the short walk across town to the museum.

They had been there before and always found it rather boring. It was full of old stuff and had very little interest in any of it until today.

The building was very large and had three floors. The first floor held lots of cabinets with old tools and weapons and bones that had been found in the local area. These were very interesting, but weren't what they were looking for. "Come on, let's go upstairs," said Martin, who had had enough of old bones, rusty old swords and guns.

"What if I stay on this floor," said Rebecca. "You and Anna can go on to the next. We can meet here later," she said, pointing at the large plan of the museum.

They quickly climbed the stairs to the second floor. This floor contained lots of stuffed animals. Anna didn't like it one bit and found them rather spooky. "I don't like this place," she said and suggested they went up to the third floor.

"Hang on!" said Martin who was very interested in a stuffed otter. It wasn't so much the otter that interested Martin, but the fact that someone had taken so much time to stuff and preserve such a fine animal. "How could they do this?" he asked.

There was no reply, Anna had gone. Oh well he thought just typical of a girl. Anna reached the third floor a little out of breath, due to the fact she'd run up the stairs away from all of the dead animals which had given her a rather sickly feeling in her stomach.

She was pleased to see that this floor was, in fact, a gallery and contained many drawings and paintings. She walked slowly past each one. Some were rather small paintings, others were just ridiculous she thought. How could you get that into a house? You would have to knock the walls down just to get them in!

She wasn't really looking at what the paintings were of. She was more interested in the colours and how big some of them were.

It was by chance that a small painting caught her eye. It was in the landscape section and clearly showed their cove with the cliff and there, clear as day, was the pathway leading up the cliff to the tunnel entrance.

She read the information card below.

PAINTING BY UNKNOWN ARTIST.

PAINTING SHOWS "SHALLOW POINT BAY."

PAINTING DATED C1600.

Was this good or what? She thought. The others will be pleased. Just as she turned to go and get the others she saw one of the museum guides. "Can you help me?" she asked.

"Yes certainly," said the guide. She was dressed in a rather posh suit and spoke in a very authorative manner.

"Where did this painting come from and how long has it been here?" Anna said pointing at the small picture.

"Well, we have very little knowledge of this painting. I don't know where it came from or how long it's been in the museum, I'm afraid,"

"Is there anyone else I could ask?" said Anna.

"No there isn't!" came the reply, with some irritation.

"Well, thank you, anyway," said Anna, who decided it would be better to get the others. She didn't like talking to grown-ups much and felt very uncomfortable being questioned about why she was so interested in this particular painting. She took one last look at the painting on the wall, making sure she remembered where it was hanging so that she could show the others.

Old books, paintings and shoes

She found Martin walking in a dream around the stuffed dead animals. She did not tell him anything other than she needed him and Rebecca to come quickly, as she had found something very interesting. They both searched the first floor and found Rebecca looking into a glass case containing the remains of clothing and old shoes.

They were very surprised to see a shoe that was the same as the one Martin had found. "Look!" said Martin. "Look it's, it's!"

"Yes," said Rebecca. "Just like the one you found."

"That's good!" said Anna, "but I've found something better!"

"What's that?" said Martin.

"Come with me and I'll show you." They followed Anna up two flights of stairs.

"Hang on!" cried Martin, who was not as fit as the two girls and was struggling to keep up.

As Anna approached the wall, displaying the landscape paintings, her heart began to beat with such force she was sure that the others must be able to hear it. Anna stopped suddenly. "It's gone!"

"What's gone?" Martin asked with a confused look on his now glowing red face.

"It has!" shouting so loud that all the other visitors turned around to see what the commotion was.

"What is it supposed to be?" Martin whispered, trying to calm Anna down.

"The painting!" cried Anna.

"What painting?" shouted Martin.

"The one of the cliff. It showed the cliff, the path and the cave!" said Anna.

"Well it's not there now is it?" shouted Martin.

"Just a minute," said Rebecca. "If Anna said it was here, then I'm sure it was. The thing that puzzles me is where is it now? And why would anyone take it?"

"There was a woman, an assistant who I spoke to about the painting," said Anna.

"I think you mean curator?" Martin said smugly.

"I don't know what you call them, but she was here and I asked her about the painting," replied Anna.

"Let's see if we can't find her. She may know what has happened to the painting," replied Anna. As Anna looked around the gallery she saw the woman she had been talking to earlier heading toward the stairs and she seemed in a hurry. "Stop!" shouted Anna, forgetting where she was.

All the other visitors turned and stared at her. How she wished she could just disappear and become invisible so that she could walk out without having so many glaring eyes looking at her.

Her call had the right affect on the woman she had stopped and glanced back at Anna. "That's her!" Anna shouted again. "Can you help us please?"

This time one of the visitors came over.

"Do you know where you are? That is not the way to behave in a museum. If you want to shout and run around like a small child then I suggest you go to a playground, not a museum!"

Anna wasn't listening. She pushed past the man and said to the others "Come on or we will lose her."

"Well," said the man "kids today."

"Yes, I agree," shouted Martin as he pushed past the man who was becoming angrier by the minute. The man made a grab for Martin's coat but was far too slow.

They caught the woman just as she reached the first floor. "Excuse me!" said Anna. The woman ignored her. "Excuse me!" Anna said again, this time grabbing the woman's arm. Once Anna had got a grip of the woman's arm she was not going to let go.

She held it as though her life depended on it. "Just what is it you want?" asked the woman, who clearly was not happy having a small child swinging on her arm.

"All I want is to ask you where the painting is," said Anna. "What are you talking about?" asked the woman.

"You know, the painting I asked you about not more than twenty minutes ago," said Anna.

"I'm sorry! But I don't have a clue what you are talking about," replied the woman.

"Yes you do! I asked you about a small painting that was on display in the gallery," shouted Anna.

"I'm sorry but I really don't know what you are talking about and if you think I'm going to stand here with a bunch of kids, discussing something that never happened then you are mistaken. Now please let go of my arm and get out of my way," said the woman, walking away.

The woman pushed past the people that had gathered and left the building. "Don't worry let her go," said Martin. "I know where she lives and I know who she's living with."

"But that's not the point," said Anna.

"I don't care who she is or where she lives, I want to know where the painting has gone?"

"Well she didn't seem too keen to tell you," said Martin.

"Well she's gone now and so has the painting," said Rebecca.

"Isn't it strange how such a small and uninteresting painting can cause someone to panic so much," she continued. "If that little painting is so important then I think there is much more to the old tunnel we've found and not just because it contains a pile of old furniture and a shoe."

All three sat on the steps leading up to the main doors to the museum. Anna was being consoled by Rebecca who could see she was upset by what had just happened. In addition to the run in with her they had all been asked to leave the museum and not to return until they had learnt to behave.

"Grown-ups!" said Martin. "It's them that need to grow up. They just don't listen. I tried to tell them what had happened but all the security guard kept saying was "I think it would be best if you left the museum.""

"So here we are with nothing to show for all our efforts. I don't know," said Rebecca.

"We've seen a shoe like the one you found. We've seen a painting showing the pathway." " And the tunnel," interrupted Anna.

"Not forgetting our new friend!" said Martin nodding his head in the direction she had left.

"Well," said Rebecca, "Let's not waste time sitting here. I think we should pay this strange woman a visit."

"Just a minute!" said Martin, "I haven't told you who she is living with and I think you may change your mind once I have."

"You know the big white house at the top of the hill on the road leading out of our village?"

"Yes," replied the girls.

"Well that's where I have seen her. I saw her leaving that house one morning. She must have been going to work or something."

"But isn't that where Mr Richardson lives?" said Rebecca.

"Correct," said Martin.

41

"I'd be very surprised if she's anything to hide," said Rebecca.

"Why?" Anna asked, feeling left out again.

"Because Mr Richardson is a policeman," they both replied.

"Policemen do strange things. Just because they wear a uniform and arrest people doesn't mean they are all whiter than white," said Rebecca.

"Get you!" said Martin.

"You sometimes say some very grown up things considering you're only ten."

"Nearly eleven," said Anna sharply.

"So!" said Rebecca.

"So what?" said Martin.

"So what are we going to do?" asked Rebecca.

"Well, I think we should go and tell someone about what we have found, and about that strange woman," said Anna.

"Hang on!" said Martin. "If we do then that will be the end to our little adventure."

"Adventure? Is that what you call it?" said Rebecca.

"Okay, what would you call it Miss Smarty Pants?" said Martin.

"Well it's, it's," stammered Rebecca.

"Well it's a pretty good adventure up to now!" Martin interrupted. "I've not had this much fun for ages. Do we have to tell anyone? We haven't done anything wrong! All we've done is made a few noises in some old museum and I don't think that will cause any problems." Rebecca looked directly at Anna who seemed very unsure about what to do.

"Okay" said Anna.

"Great," said Martin. "Let's get home and we'll meet tomorrow morning early."

"The three of them sat very quiet on the bus as it made its way back to the village. Once off the bus Martin had little to say other than "see you tomorrow, 9:30 my place," he called to the girls as he ran towards his house.

"See you tomorrow then, Anna," said Rebecca.

"Yes sure, I'll call for you on the way to Martin's," replied Anna.

Rebecca was dressed and waiting for Anna, gazing through the window, waiting for sight of her. Suddenly, she felt a cold chill run through her body. It couldn't be could it? Surely not! There, walking up the street in the direction of Rebecca's home was the very woman who had run out of the museum the day before.

Rebecca closed the curtains quickly and sank to her knees. It wasn't long before there was a loud knock on the front door. Rebecca could hear the muffled voices coming from the hall. She held her breath trying hard to hear what was being said. Before she could do anything the lounge door opened. "Rebecca, there's someone here to see you." There she stood! The very woman who had been so angry, the previous day, at the museum. She was surely going to say something about the trouble they had caused. But no!

The woman reached out her hand and said, "Morning, Rebecca. My name is Susan Green."

"I've just been telling your mother," she continued, "how interested you were in a painting hanging in the local museum. Once I had found out you lived in the very same village as me, I just had to come and give you this." She reached inside the large coat she was wearing and pulled out a book. "This has information about this area. You'll find lots about the cliffs and coves. That was what you wanted?" Rebecca was not sure if she should be scared or grateful? She was confused and frightened. "If ever you want to come and see me about anything to do with local history, please come over to my house, any time."

Susan Green looked down at her watch. "Well, I must be off! And don't forget, Rebecca, if ever you want anything just ask," she said. Rebecca was still shaking when her mother returned having seen Susan Green to the door.

"Well, wasn't that nice of Mrs Green," she said as she entered the room.

"Yes, mum," said Rebecca.

"Well, I think it is! She doesn't even know you," her mother continued.

As Rebecca watched Susan Green drive away she saw Anna coming down the road. "Okay if I go now mum? Only Martin and Anna will be waiting."

"Yes, but I want to know more about that painting and why you went all the way to the museum, without letting me or your dad know?"

"I'll tell you later," she called back to her mother as she closed the front door with a bang.

Unexpected visitor

"You look terrible! Just seen a ghost or something?" said Anna.

"Worse than that! I just had a visit from our new friend from the museum."

"What, that woman?"

"Yes that woman!"

"When did she call? Asked Anna with panic in her voice.

"Just!" replied Rebecca.

"What, just now?" said Anna, this time with a hint of fear in her voice.

"Yes! She gave me this."

Rebecca held out the book. "What is it?" asked Anna.

I haven't looked at it yet," said Rebecca. "I thought I should wait until we get to Martin's. Come on let's get over there."

Having rung the door bell at least ten times Anna and Rebecca were about to turn to leave when the front door of Martin's house swung open.

As it did, the voices grew louder. "Well, thank you very much," said Martin's dad. "Oh, hello you two, sorry I didn't answer sooner but we've just been discussing your little trip to the museum." Anna moved to hide behind Rebecca.

"Well, this must be the other two we were just talking about," said Mrs Green.

"Yes," said Martin's dad. "These are the other members of their little gang."

"See you all again soon," said Mrs Green as she left.

"Come on in," said Martin's dad. "You'll find him in his room. Don't forget your shoes," he called as the two girls ran for the stairs.

They joined Martin in his room. He was sat holding a book. "What's that?" asked Rebecca half knowing what the answer was going to be.

"Mrs Green gave it to me. She said she'd already met you."

He reached over and tugged on Rebecca's jumper. "She has!" said Rebecca. They all sat on Martin's bed looking at the two books.

There were lots of old photographs and sketches in them. And as Mrs Green had said there was lots of information about the cliffs and coves where the three of them had played for many years.

"Why would she want us to have these books?" wondered Martin.

"Why would she come to our homes if she was so angry yesterday?" said Rebecca.

"And why is she being so helpful when yesterday she told us she knew nothing and didn't understand what we were talking about?" said Anna.

After they had all had a drink they sat looking out of Martin's bedroom window. "I just don't get it." said Martin. "Why is she being so helpful now?"

"I don't know," said Anna "but I don't like her."

"I think she is up to something," said Rebecca. "Maybe we should go and see her," she continued.

"You can go on your own," said Anna.

"No, I think we should all go," said Martin. "She can't do anything if we are all there."

"I don't know," said Anna, again.

"Come on, Anna! I wouldn't ask you if I thought it was dangerous," said Martin.

"Come on, say yes!" Rebecca pleaded. She didn't want Martin or Anna to think she was scared even though she was.

Hard to believe

All three set off up the road towards the big white house. As they entered the garden they could see Mrs Green through the kitchen window.

Martin rang the door bell. It wasn't long before Mrs Green was opening the door. "Here goes," said Martin just as the door began opening.

"Well, hello again," said Mrs Green. "Do come in, I'm about to have some tea, would you like one?"

"No thank you," they all said at once.

"Well a drink of something else? Pop, squash, coke?" Mrs Green asked.

"Nothing for me," said Martin, "I've just had a drink."

"So have we," said the others, feeling very awkward.

"Come on, let's go into the study. I've something to show you. Oh, I'm Mrs Green, Susan." She turned and said to Anna, reaching out a hand to shake. Anna did not respond.   There is no way she's holding my hand. Thought Anna and kept her hands firmly in her pockets.

As they entered the study the smell of leather and polish hit them. It smelt old, like the museum.

"This is my favourite place," said Susan Green. "This is where I come when I need to recharge my batteries."

"Blimey, she's a robot," thought Martin.   "No she couldn't be. She moved too well to be a robot. Stop day dreaming," he told himself and brought his thoughts back to the matter in hand.

"Well I can't tell you how glad I am you came up. I couldn't say anything when I visited your homes," began Mrs Green.

"You see, what I'm about to tell you must never be told to anyone else. Can I trust you?" she asked the children.

"Can we trust you?" asked Rebecca?

"Well, let's start by me sharing something with you," replied Mrs Green.

"Please sit down." She pointed to a long leather settee. All three sat huddled at one end.

"Well, let's start with what you know!" she continued. "You tell me if I've got it wrong."

"Three days ago you found a path cut into the cliff face? Correct?" They all nodded yes.

"You also found a tunnel at the end of the path? Correct?" They all nodded again.

"You've all been into the tunnel?" They all nodded in silence again.

"Well, what do you think it is?" she said looking at Martin.

"Don't know!" he replied.

"How about you Anna?"

"Just a load of old junk and tables!" said Anna.

"So you've been down to the great hall? Well that must have been a real adventure, I am sure!"

Martin looked at Anna. He was not pleased. He cut in "we don't know anything!"

"But you do!" said Susan Green, looking at him with eyes of steel.

"You don't know about the great hall."

"No, we don't. We didn't see anything other than a load of old tables and chairs," insisted Martin.

"Well, what do you think they were doing there?"

"I don't know," Martin replied.

"I believe you!" said Mrs Green.

Susan walked over to the arm chair next to the fire. Having made herself comfortable, she looked across at the children and spoke in a very gentle manner.

"Come on, let's all calm down. I'm not going to hurt you. I just have to be sure I can trust you."

Susan Green stood, suddenly. She paused for a moment looking at the children, then left the room. She didn't say anything. The room fell into total silence.

This made all of them feel very uneasy. "What do you think she is doing?" whispered Anna. There was no reply from the others.

"Bet her name isn't really Susan Green!" said Martin.

They all jumped, as the sound of something being dragged along the floor caught their attention.

"What's she doing now?" said Anna, who was sat with her back to the door.

"Don't know. I can't see," replied Martin.

It wasn't long before Susan Green joined them. She was pulling a rather large trunk into the room. "Sorry I took so long!" she said as she began undoing the latches on the trunk. "It's been a long time since this was opened," she said as she continued releasing even more latches.

As the lid fell open the contents filled the air with the smell of sea spray and old rope. "Hang on!" said Martin. "What are you doing?"

"Nothing for you to be afraid of," said Mrs Green.

"I just want to show you something that I think you will find very interesting, and, I am sure you would like to know why I am so keen to find out what you know about the mine."

The trunk contained what appeared to be bundles of old clothes. And a few cords.

"Well!" said Rebecca, who was not too impressed with the trunks contents.

"Well," said Mrs Green. "What do you think they are?"

"A load of old rubbish," said Martin.

"They may look like that to you, but, what would you say if I told you they were over a thousand years old?"

"Don't be silly!" said Anna. "Nothing lasts that long."

"Well these have and there are more in the mine."

"Really!" said Martin. "If these things are that old, why aren't they in your precious museum?"

"Well that's the problem. These are not ordinary clothes." Susan held one up in her hands. Opening it out on top of the trunk she continued. "There is something very special about them."

"Oh really. What's that?" asked Martin.

"Well, Nothing."

"Nothing!" Martin exclaimed.

"Nothing!" came the response for the second time.

"Why are you showing us then?" Rebecca asked with a very puzzled look on her face.

"Because of that! There is nothing" said Mrs Green.

"What are you going on about?" said Martin.

"Stop!" interrupted Rebecca. "This is crazy. You come to our homes, you give us books, and you pretend you don't know us in the museum, now you show us an old trunk containing clothes that you claim to be a thousand years old. You then try to tell us there is nothing special about them."

"Yes! That's correct. Let me explain," said Mrs Green.

"This should be good." It was Martin's turn to interrupt.

"Well, when you look at these clothes they don't look like anything special. But what if I was to tell you that this one was once worn by a prince." Mrs Green reached into the trunk and held up a gown.

"What did he wear that for? Gardening?" laughed Martin.

"No. This was a very special gown worn only on special occasions, council meetings, celebrations and weddings, that sort of thing."

"So!" said Anna, who had now walked over to the trunk so she could see inside.

"What about this one?" Anna reached into the trunk and held up another of the old gowns.

"That one was worn by a princess."

"Really!" said Anna who was feeling excited at the thought that a princess had worn this very gown.

"Well, they don't look like the sort of clothes a prince and princess would wear," said Martin.

"You can't see what I mean but you will," said Mrs Green, "you will."

"I said there was nothing special," continued Mrs Green. "That's it nothing."

"Nothing!" said Martin. "Here we go again. What do you mean? Nothing?"

"Nothing! Just that, nothing. Many years ago the people that lived in this area found something that would change the way they lived. They didn't know what it was called so over the years it became known as nothing," explained Mrs Green.

"Why?" asked Rebecca who had been listening to all the discussions and had been intrigued by the idea that there were people living here more than a thousand years ago.

"Well, a long time ago the people had been working underground digging iron ore from the rocks. It was during this mining that they discovered a very strange substance.

"No one knew what it was or what to call it." "What was it like?" asked Anna.

"If you can imagine the brightest diamond or the deepest sapphires or most colourful opal, they would not outshine nothing."

"It was not only bright but it could be moulded in your hands, it could be sewn into clothing and made into jewellery. Many kept it locked away in case someone should try to take it."

"Many had large amounts of it. All miners gathered nothing as they worked away underground."

"Hang on!" cried Martin, who could not contain himself any longer. "Hang on!" he said again. "If there was so much of this stuff."

"Nothing!" interrupted Anna. "Where is it now?"

"There is still a little in these parts but nothing like as much as there was," answered Mrs Green.

"Really. So what happened to it?" asked Anna.

"Well now, this is where things get interesting," continued Mrs Green.

"There was just one problem with nothing. It was just one of nature's many wonders!"

"It was one of those things that always made you ask why. I always think of it as the law of paradise."

"Law of paradise?" chirped Rebecca.

"Yes, the paradise law," said Mrs Green.

"Let's take a beautiful island paradise as an example, with its lovely beaches, warm sun, deep blue sea, everyone's dream. Unfortunately, the opposite also applies. They have some of the worst storms, hurricanes and even plagues."

"So, as wonderful a paradise may be, it can be equally bad. The paradise you had one minute can be gone the next."

"That's the thing with nothing. So long as you keep it below ground it's fine. But bring it to the surface and hey presto, it's gone!"

"Gone?" said Martin, who by now was more confused than ever.

"And how did you become one of the keepers?" asked Martin.

"Mr Richardson and I are from a long line of keepers. My name is not Susan Green. That's just a name I use so as not to draw attention."

"Told you," said Martin, looking across at the others as if to say, "I knew all the time."

"Martin!" said Rebecca, "Shut up."

"My real name is Shangala Breanon, which means shining beacon in your language," explained Susan Green.

"And Mr Richardson?" asked Anna.

"Well his name is Majula Rigalon, which means Majestic Regal one."

"So what are you doing here?" asked Martin.

"We are here to protect what is left of nothing," said Mrs Green.

"So now you know a lot more than before. It's up to you now. I've told you all about nothing. I hope I can trust you to keep it to yourselves," said Mrs Green as she packed the clothes and map back in the chest.

As the three of them walked home there was very little said, it was only when they reached Anna's house and sat on the porch that Martin spoke.

"I don't think we should tell anyone about this morning."

"Why not?" asked Anna.

"Because if we tell anyone they will only want to go and see for themselves and we won't be allowed to go anymore."

"I agree," said Rebecca. "We don't have to tell anyone and we're not in any trouble, so do we all agree we tell no one?"

Return to darkness

It was three in the afternoon when they all met again. Anna had been sitting out on her porch for a while and had been getting worried about the others, as Rebecca and Martin approached, she ran to join them. "Where have you been?" she asked.

"We had to have something to eat!" said Martin.

"I know," said Anna "but there is such thing as the phone. You're always saying how good yours is! I can call anywhere in the world, you said! I can call anyone with this, you said!"

"I know," said Martin "don't go on."

"You try sitting here with everything going through your head," said Anna.

"Like what?" said Martin.

"Like...like...you know what I mean," shouted Anna.

"Come on," said Rebecca "we have a lot to think about." They made their way down to the beach. It was chilly now as the wind had got up and the sun was beginning to sink behind the thick, black clouds.

"Looks like rain," said Rebecca.

"Not for a while," said Martin holding his hand in the air as if he were checking for some sign of rain.

"Let's go to the entrance before it does," said Anna.

As they sat in the dim light, they all felt a strange kind of warmth, almost a welcome feeling.

"I'm not sure we've been told all that there is to know about what happened here. Why did Susan Green decide to tell us what was behind the missing picture and the trunk full of clothes? She could have just told our parents that we had been doing something dangerous or had misbehaved in the museum. But no, she has got us in her house and then filled our heads with some strange tale of her being a princess and guardian of some ancient treasure."

"Don't you believe her?" said Anna. "I'm not saying what she told us isn't true, but it's the way she wants us to keep it to ourselves."

"Surely, if this Nothing is so amazing she would want to put it to good use. Maybe it could be the cure for a cold or some of the terrible diseases we have no cures for. I don't know, why would she not want to help the people she now loves and lives with?"

Martin stood. He pointed his finger down the tunnel and looking back at the two girls said "I'm going back down there! It's a big hole and someone dug it, it didn't just appear."

"I'm not sure I want to," said Anna. "I'm too scared to go back in, it's a long way and anything could happen. No one knows we are here and if we get stuck down there we will never be found."

"Okay," said Martin. "I'm not saying we go down now but maybe tomorrow or even the next day."

"Only if we all agree," said Rebecca.

"I think that's a great idea," said Anna dabbing the tears away from her eyes.

They went back out into the damp late afternoon air and walked back to Anna's house. "Do you want to come in and watch TV?" asked Anna. "No," said Martin "I want some time to think. We need to decide what we do next and how we can be safe."

It was about 3am and Martin had not been able to sleep. As hard as he tried he could not stop thinking about the tale Susan Green had told them all.

He wanted to believe her and was now wishing he'd never found the entrance to the mine and that he could return to just digging holes on the beach and swimming in the sea, with his two, dear friends.

He hoped he had not put any of them in danger because of some foolish need to go searching for some magical treasure.

When he awoke it was with a jump. Where was he? What had happened to make him feel so cold? His bed was wet with sweat and his eyes ached.

At 10.30am he and Rebecca would meet at Anna's house, as agreed the night before. And sure enough, as he walked into Anna's garden, there sat the two girls.

"You look terrible," said Rebecca.

"You don't look so good yourself," Martin replied.

"No, I couldn't sleep and I felt as if I'd got the flu."

"Me too," said Anna. "That's just like I felt when I woke this morning."

"Maybe we've all got a chill or cold or something. Well whatever it is I don't feel too bad now, and I've worked out how we can go back to the mine and also be safe should anything happen," said Martin.

By the time they'd reached the entrance to the mine, Martin had told the girls of his plan and they were feeling much better about entering the mine again.

As they entered a strange feeling came over each of them. No one said anything but it was so obvious that something had happened as they were all now feeling fresh and well. The aching had gone. The legs that had felt like lead only minutes before, felt completely okay.

They followed the passage that they had now grown to know. Having made good progress, they were now climbing down the vertical ladder attached to the shaft's wall.

As they reached the point where Martin had to jump into the darkness, he turned on the large lamp he had brought from his father's workshop. "See for miles with this baby," he said, as he turned it on. It was a very powerful lamp and lit the whole shaft above them. There was a flutter as a few birds that had roosted in the shaft, headed for the outside world and daylight.

Martin uncoiled the rope from around his shoulders and threw it down beyond the end of the ladder. "You go first," he said to Rebecca. "I'll stay here and lower Anna down to you. Don't want you falling off and breaking anything." He swung the torch, lighting Anna's face with its bright beam.

"Don't do that," she said, holding a hand up in front of her eyes.

"Hey! I'm still down here," called Rebecca, from below.

"Sorry," said Martin. He shone the torch back down the shaft. "Here hold this a minute." He passed the torch to Anna so he could secure the rope around her waist. He showed her how to hold onto the rope as he lowered her down to join Rebecca.

Once Rebecca had removed the rope from Anna's waist, Martin quickly joined them. "That was easy," he said rubbing his hands together.

"Never knew you were that strong," said Anna.

"Neither did I," he replied.

Now all three stood looking up at the shaft they had all dropped down so willingly. The silence was broken when Martin spoke. "How you feeling?" he asked.

"Amazing," answered Rebecca. "And you?" she said, looking at Anna.

"I'm fine. I don't even feel scared anymore," said Anna.

"Well, I don't know what it is," said Martin "but I think we are all feeling a bit odd today."

Anna laughed out loud, "you're odd every day!" she said, pointing a finger at Martin.

"That's me," he said, with a grin on his face. They stumbled over the broken remains of tables and chairs. It was hard to count how many there were, but they appeared to go on forever. "This was some kind of party," he said out loud.

"Quiet!" Rebecca said suddenly. "Can you hear that?"

"What?" asked Anna.

"That!" said Rebecca, as they stood motionless; they could hear a very strange sound coming from the far end of the hall.

The sound of music

The sound was very similar to that made by a child's toy piano or an old wind up music box.

It was that sort of noise but it seemed to ring out for a very long time. Each note ringing out and then gradually fading as the next note sounded out.

"That's wonderful!" said Anna. "Let's go and see what it is," and with the feeling of fear long gone they were now rushing toward the source of the sound. As they arrived at the end of the hall the noise became louder and in front of them stood a great black wall. It shone like a highly polished car.

As they moved closer to the shining black wall the louder the sound became. It was now clear that the wall was running with water.

"Well, that's why it shines so much," said Martin. "There's a complete sheet of water running over the black rock."

Luckily, Martin had decided to shine the lamp onto the floor. "Stop!" Martin shouted. They all found themselves standing on the edge of a very deep ravine. "That was close," said Martin "a few more steps and one of us, or even all of us would have been over the edge and who knows where."

They all dropped to the floor, hugging the rough surface as if their lives depended on it. Gradually, they crawled to the edge and looked down into the bottomless void. The water glinted in the lamp's beam. The site that met them was one of hundreds of jet black crystals protruding from the face of the black wall, each glistening in the light. "Are they black diamonds?" said Rebecca.

"Not sure," said Martin, wanting to be the voice of authority again.

"They may be," said Anna. "They do exist, I've read about them in my mum's books."

"Well done!" said Rebecca. "See, Martin, you're not the only one who knows stuff."

"I didn't say she was wrong did I!" said Martin, still focused on the black spikes pointing out into the water flow.

"I think I see what's making the noise," said Rebecca, clearing her throat. They all lay watching the water run down the wall. The silence only being interrupted by the noise coming from the wall itself. It was a beautiful clear ringing sound.

"I've got it!" Rebecca said excitedly. "Look," she pointed down into the gully. "The water that is running down the wall is filling that trough attached to that large beam. Each time it fills it lifts the beam like a giant seesaw, which empties at the top. This causes the beam to drop and as it does the other end throws water onto the crystals, making them ring and I suppose that the noise is amplified by this great black wall in front of us."

"Like a tuning fork on a wooden table," said Anna. The other two looked at Anna in amazement.

"Where did that come from?" said Martin.

"I know stuff!" came the reply, as Anna looked back down into the blackness.

"Come on then, we need to get moving if we're going to find anything before this lamp fails," said Rebecca. They had now grown used to the sound of the tinkling made by the wall of water, and had only found more broken tables and chairs.

"It's time we left," said Martin, who was still feeling very good, both inside and out.

He found he could move much faster than first thing that morning and was surprised to find little Anna pushing past him to climb the rope back up to the ladder. "Time for dinner?" Martin was rubbing his stomach as if he'd not eaten for days.

"Lunch?" said Anna who was now beginning to annoy both Rebecca and Martin. "What's wrong?" she said as they both glared at her. "Well it is lunch. Mum said we have lunch at one and dinner at six, so I must be right."

"You are," laughed Rebecca as she placed the last bit of broken branch across the entrance to the mine. They all linked arms and made their way back along the track they had travelled earlier that day.

As they neared Anna's house they were puzzled by the sound of voices coming from the back garden. "I'm sorry I couldn't help. I don't know where they are." It was Anna's mum's voice they could hear and before they could do anything they were met by Susan Green as she came around the corner of the house.

"Oh, hello," she said smiling. "I've just been chatting to your mum," she said, looking at Anna and reaching out her hand. "I told her you've been up to the house and that I'd shown you some of the old antiques I keep at home."

"I was wondering," she continued, "if you would like to come up tomorrow as I am not working, due to repairs being done at the museum."

"Well! Say thank you!" said Anna's mum. "I'm sure they will all love having something to do. Nothing much happens around here."

Martin looked at Rebecca willing her to say something, hoping one of them would come up with an excuse not to go.

"Thank you," said Anna, not wishing to appear ungrateful.

"Shall we say ten tomorrow?" said Mrs Green.

"Thank you so much," said Anna's mum as she walked Susan Green to the gate.

"Maybe you can tell us about the water wall," called Anna. Susan Green turned quickly and stared at Anna.

"I'm sure there are many things to talk about. Sounds very interesting. Water walls indeed," said Anna's mum.

"See you around ten," said Mrs Green.

Martin sank onto the front door step. "Why did you say that?"

"I don't know," replied Anna. "I just wanted to say something to get rid of her. Did you see the look on her face. I bet she can't wait until ten tomorrow."

"We can always just not go," said Rebecca.

"What and have her back down here, telling our parents we've been trespassing and causing trouble at the museum," muttered Martin.

Three dangerous people

Susan Green greeted them all as they approached her front door. "Come in!" she said smiling. "Please go through into the kitchen you know the way." Anna was the last to enter still not sure what would happen next.

The door slammed behind them. "Sorry it slipped out of my hand," said Susan Green, still smiling.

There were voices coming from the kitchen. "Is it ok to go in?" said Martin, looking back at Susan.

"Yes, please go in. There is nothing to worry about." All three were panicking inside. What should they do? There was no way past Susan to the front door and the only way of reaching the back door was through the kitchen.

When they entered they found Mr Richardson and a stranger sitting at the table each holding a mug of hot tea. "Want some?" said Mr Richardson. "It's fresh!"

"Yes please!" said Anna, without hesitation. She loved her tea and was not about to miss an opportunity to have one.

Everyone was now sitting around the large wooden table. Susan Green had returned with the old map and was spreading it out on top of the table. "Before we discuss this thing," she said, pointing at the map, "let me introduce Roger or should I say PC Golding."

Rebecca wanted to interrupt. Bet that's not his real name, she wanted to say, but thought she would wait.

The very sound of PC sent a shiver through all three of them. Why was he here? What did he want? And, were they in trouble?

The sound of Susan's voice cut through the air like a knife through butter, sharp and to the point.

"Trespassing!" she said. "Private property!" she said. "Breaking the law!" she said.

"Well, let's see first," said PC Golding. He had turned the map to face him so that he could get a clearer view.

"Here's the mine and you can see clearly the land it is on." Susan was standing over the map and running her finger around the point on the map where the entrance to the mine was located.

"I don't want you three getting into trouble just because you're having a bit of fun searching the old mine. It's a very dangerous place and we don't want you getting hurt, do we. Apart from the fact that it's on private land and makes it even more important that you stay out of the mine."

"It's for your own safety," she said, smiling all the time.

"Why didn't you say that the other day when you showed us all that stuff?" said Rebecca.

"Well, I thought you'd just found the entrance but when you said you reached the water wall, I knew you must have gone in and entered the great hall."

"The great hall?" interrupted PC Golding. "It's a large chamber that's a fair way from the entrance. I'm amazed you haven't been hurt already. It's a very dangerous place and no one has been in there for years."

"So what are you saying?" asked Martin who was now becoming more scared by the minute.

"I'm saying keep out of the mine for your own safety, and, also, you could find yourself in trouble for trespassing," said PC Golding.

"Why is he here?" Martin said, pointing at PC Golding.

"I just wanted to be sure that what I am saying is correct and that you understand that it is not me, not wanting you to go there. It's not your land and it's dangerous!"

Martin felt even colder although there was a fire burning in the hearth. The map was now being studied closely by PC Golding and Mr Richardson, as Susan pointed out the entrance location and how far the great hall was from the entrance.

As the others studied the map, Martin was trying to pull his mobile phone from his pocket. If he could get it without them seeing, he could call his home. He finally managed to get it out and held it under the table where only he could see it. He managed to set the phone to silent and began dialling.

Suddenly, he realised that Susan Green was staring straight at him. "Well," she said, "do you understand how important it is that you stay away?"

As each word reached his ears they jarred in his head. Like someone hitting him on top of the head with a very large book.

Susan Green stood up and went over to the kettle and made fresh tea for PC Golding and Mr Richardson. "You sure you don't want a drink?" she said still looking down at the teacups. Everyone turned to look in her direction. "Oh I have made you two fresh brews, I meant the children.

"No thanks," the three of them said together. Martin's head was spinning. Why is she so keen to keep us away? Why is it so important?

PC Golding spoke, "Well," he said, "Let's take a closer look and see if we can make sense of this?"

"This map, it's very old and there are no roads or fences. I guess when it was drawn up all those years ago, no one even owned the land. That's not to say someone doesn't today."

"That's not what's bothering me, I am concerned that you lot are roaming around down this old mine without permission or the right equipment. Bet all you had was a torch?"

"We had two actually!" said Anna.

"There you go. Just what you would expect from kids," said PC Golding. Martin looked at Anna. He didn't have to say anything. She knew from the look on his face that she should have kept quiet.

"So as long as you agree not to go down the mine again, I will consider the matter closed. Be sure I will be keeping an eye on the old mine and once I have established who owns the land, I will contact them and get the entrance secured," said the policeman.

He stood and shook Mr Richardson's hand. "I'll have to be going, lots to do back at the station. I'll get back to you once I have completed my investigation.

Susan showed PC Golding to the front door. As he reached for the handle PC Golding turned and began to raise his voice. "What if they find their way through the wall? You better be sure they stay away!"

Susan closed the door and returned to the kitchen. "Well, who's for tea?" "No thanks," they all replied. Martin looked at the clock on the wall it was 11:30.

An hour had passed so quickly. "I think we should be getting back home, mum's cooking dinner for us."

"She is?" the words stumbled out of Anna's mouth between splutters and gulps.

Martin just looked at the table.

"Ok, I won't keep you any longer. You do know I am doing this for your own good and I want you to be safe. I don't want to read about three lovely children going missing."

"Thank you," said Rebecca. "We better get going or we'll be late."

As the door closed behind them Martin said, "don't run, walk slowly. I don't want her thinking she's scared us and running away from her house would only make her think we know more than we have told her."

They jumped when Martin's mobile went off in his pocket. Martin pressed the answer button. A strange voice was on the other end. "Stay away! Stay away or you will regret ever finding the mine." The line went dead.

Martin's face was now trembling and growing very pale. "What is it?" said Rebecca.

"I don't know?"

"What do you mean, you don't know?"

"I don't," he said. "All they said was 'stay away' then hung up.

"They?" said Anna.

"OK he said 'stay away'."

"Did you recognise the voice?"

"No one I know," came the reply.

Martin's heart had slowed to a reasonable rate by the time they had reached Anna's garden gate. "Coming in?" she said. "There's no one home until later. Mum's gone to see Gran and won't be home until this afternoon." It wasn't long before they were all sat at the kitchen table, eating buttered toast with a glass of orange juice.

"There's much more to that mine than the Princess of darkness is letting on," said Martin.

"Princess of darkness?" said Anna.

"You know who I mean, Susan flipping Green!"

"Why is she being so protective we've said we won't tell anyone else about the mine? It's our secret!" said Anna.

"Was!" said Martin. "We have already shared what we know with Susan Green and she is bound to have told Mr Richardson."

"He didn't say a word up there," said Martin, nodding his head in the direction of Susan Green's house. "Why do you think that was?"

"Don't know?" said Martin.

"It's all very strange and that is why I am sure there is more to that mine." They all sat in silence as if frozen in time.

"Hang on!" said Martin. "Let's look back at the last week." Martin was now pacing around the kitchen. "We had the storm. We found the path. We found the entrance to the mine."

"We found the shoe!" interrupted Anna.

"We entered the tunnel and found the shaft. We found a very large cavern."

"The great hall" interrupted Anna again.

"Yes, that as well," said Martin. He then said "sorry". He could see he had hurt Anna with his blunt remark. "The great hall he continued. We go to the museum and find a very old painting showing the path and entrance to the mine, that we know had been removed by Susan Green, who then lets us into her home to show us some old clothes and a map. Then she tells us a fantastic story about an ancient person who created the mine, searching for Nothing. And then she tries to buy our silence and asks us to keep everything we heard a secret."

"When that doesn't work she asks us back to the house and tells us that it is for our own good. She asks us to stop going to the mine."

"Now we have the police involved, if that is what he was? Said Martin, now holding his head in his hands.

"All this is making my head spin. In fact I feel rubbish again."

"Me too," said Anna.

"Well, I'm not feeling too good myself," said Rebecca. "Anyone want a drink? I tell you there's something not right about Susan Green," she continued.

"I think she is nice," said Anna. "She's very kind, didn't she tell us her secret and show us all those old clothes and the old map?"

"That could have come from anywhere," interrupted Rebecca.

"Yes, true, but she didn't have to tell us anything and could have gone to our parents or to the police," said Anna.

Martin stood. "Hang on!" he said. "Why hasn't she done that? It would be very simple to just tell our parents. I tell you she wants to keep the mine a secret and I think she thought by showing us what she had, and filling our heads with an amazing fantasy story, we would be only too happy to keep her secret.

"She was only dealing with a bunch of kids after all. Well this kid is sure there is a lot more to that mine."

"There's no time to waste. We need to get back down there before the entrance is blocked off or we'll never know what truly interests Mrs Green and her friends."

"Let's not be stupid," said Rebecca. "Don't we need more ropes, torches and stuff?"

Martin looked across at Rebecca. "Look," he said, "I think I know who was on the phone. I knew I'd heard the voice before! I wasn't sure at first? It's just come to me who it is and where I'd heard it."

"Who was it?" said Anna, becoming very irritated.

"It was Mr Richardson. Remember when we met him on the beach with his dog. He only spoke briefly but I am pretty sure it was his voice on the end of my phone," answered Martin.

"Maybe that was why he was on the beach," said Anna moving closer to Martin and grabbing his arm. "What do we do now?"

Martin looked down at the table. "I think I may have something that will help."

He pulled his phone from his pocket. "I've got something here that could be useful."

"Your phone?" said Anna. "Who you going to call?"

"No one. It's what I have on the phone!" he continued. "When you lot were busy deciding if you wanted a drink or not I took a photo of the map."

"How? They would have noticed, surely."

"Remember, Susan asked if you wanted a drink and everyone turned to look at her. That's when I took it.

Lucky for me the flash was off. I just hope it's come out," he said, waving the phone in front of Anna's face.

"Stop it, Martin," said Rebecca.

"Look then! See if it's on there." Martin opened the phone and selected 'review'. "Wow!" came the response, as the image appeared.

"What is it?" said Rebecca.

"Fantastic," he said.

"What is?" cried Anna.

"The photo is perfect! I couldn't have got a better one if I had tried," said Martin.

"Come on you two, let's get over to my place." Martin was already out of the door and at the garden gate before Anna had chance to close the door and lock it.

"Wait for me," she cried. The words were wasted on Martin. He was now way ahead of the girls who had to run to catch up.

Martin stood waiting for them to catch up. "I'll go in and print this off," he said, holding his phone above his head. "You wait here and I'll be back as quick as I can."

The girls sat on the door step and watched the traffic pass. "Quick!" said Anna, grabbing Rebecca's hand and pulling her to her feet. "Come on, this way." As Anna turned she tripped over a plant pot next to the steps, which sent them both tumbling to the ground.

"That was close!" cried Anna.

"What was close?" said Rebecca, rubbing her knees.

"That was Susan Green's car that just went past. I'm sure they were looking for us. It was only moving slowly so I guess they've been trying to find us."

"Well done" said Rebecca, squeezing Anna's shoulder.

Martin was very surprised to find the step empty when he came out of the front door. "Over here!" He turned to see the girls crouching behind the rose bushes. "Quick!"

"What's up?" he said as he knelt down beside Anna.

"It's Susan Green. She just drove past."

"What's wrong with that?" asked Martin.

"She was driving very slowly and the other two were in the car with her. I think they were looking for us," said Anna, pulling the others down lower.

"Ok," said Martin, "let's get out of here."

After running from Martin's house they all collapsed, gasping for air. "Here," said Martin holding up three copies of the map. "Take a look at these and you'll see why Miss Green is so keen to keep us away."

The girls studied the copies. "I'm sorry Martin, but I don't see what it is you're so excited about," said Rebecca.

"There," he said pointing down at his copy that he'd placed on the ground. "There," he said again sounding a little irritated.

"Ok," said Rebecca. "It's not our fault Sherlock!"

"Well, can't you see it?" cried Martin.

"What?" said both girls.

"There, right there!" his finger was now being pushed into the paper.

"It's not the map that's important, it's that!" Under his finger was a small diagram. "Look, it's a plan of the mine. This isn't just a map of the mines location, it's also a detailed plan of the mine itself."

"So, we've got a map and a plan of the mine," said Rebecca.

"Yes. But look here!" Martin's finger was being buried into the paper again. "There's the black wall and look! Here's another passage."

"Yes. How does that tell us any more than we already know?" asked Anna.

"Look where it is! It is right behind the black wall," said Martin.

"How do you get in there?" said Rebecca.

"I'm not sure but I'm sure if we can get into the other passage way we will find more than just nothing!"

A forced return

Martin stood and looked at his phone. "3:30" he said. "I don't think there's enough time to do anything today. We all have to be home for supper."

"Dinner!" said Anna.

"Ok, whatever!" said Martin in his I told you so voice.

"If we get going first thing tomorrow, we can spend all day at the mine," said Martin.

"Take a packed lunch," said Rebecca.

"That's an idea. We can tell our parents we're having a picnic on the beach. They won't suspect a thing, as we're always doing it anyway. Great now let's decide what we need."

They all sat in a circle deciding what to take. "I'll bring my lamp," said Anna "It's better than a torch. And I know my Dad's got a very long rope in the garage. Gloves would be good and don't forget your boots."

Martin's phone rang. He answered.

"Hello! Sorry Mum! Forgot! Ok."

"What's wrong?" Anna asked.

"Nothing. It's getting late and mum wanted to know where I was." Martin opened his phone. "It's gone 5," he said snapping it shut. "Come on, we have to go."

He stood and helped Anna to her feet. As they reached Anna's gate Martin turned to the girls.

"Ok, tomorrow at nine, here."

"Yes." They both replied "and don't forget torches, boots and gloves."

"And the map," said Rebecca, waving her copy.

"Well, yes. That as well," said Martin. "If you think of anything else, bring it."

"Once we're down there we have to find out what's behind that wall," said Rebecca.

"And I don't think it will be long before the entrance is closed off," said Anna as she entered the front door.

"Hello" she called closing it behind her.

"In here," came the reply. It was her mum calling from the kitchen. What a relief to find her mother alone.

"Hello, mum!" she said, as she washed her hands at the sink. "Where have you been all day?"

"That Mrs Green's been here. She said she wanted to explain about the picture you were interested in at the museum."

Anna's mum was busy preparing dinner. She hadn't looked up from the cooker and continued to stir the contents of the pan.

"When did she call?" Anna asked, trying hard not to sound too bothered, even though every panic button on her head was being pressed at once.

"Not sure. Must have been around two thirty ish?"

Well that confirms it! She was looking for us and must have come back to the house after they had all run off to avoid her and her friends seeing them.

"Yes," her mother continued, "about 2:30 because I hadn't started this lot."

Anna's mum waved her hands over top of the pans now steaming away on top of the cooker.

"Just need to pop upstairs." Anna had reached her parent's bedroom as her mother responded.

"Ok, be quick, your dad will be in and he likes his dinner ready on the table."

Anna closed the door gently and then lifted the phone from its charger. She dialled Martin's number. "Please pick up, please pick up," she mumbled to herself.

"Hello." It wasn't Martin. "Hello, can I help you? Hello?" the phone went dead.

Anna replaced the phone and returned to the kitchen.

"Come here," her dad demanded as she entered the kitchen. He gave her a hug. "You're still not too big for one of these," he said pinching the tip of her nose.

Anna sat in her place at the table. Her parents chatted about what they had done during the day.

All Anna heard were random words, her mind was whirling with thoughts of Susan Green knocking on the door and what she should do if she did!

The next thing she felt was her dad shaking her arm. "Well," he was saying, "what's this picture then?"

"Sorry, what?"

"What was the picture at the museum?"

"Oh, nothing really! It was a very old painting that showed the beach as it was over one hundred years ago."

"A local artist had painted it and I'd asked where he was from and Mrs Green had said she would look into it."

"Wow!" said Anna's dad, sitting back in his chair. "That's very kind of her to come here to let you know she found something."

"Maybe we can go to the museum tomorrow? I'm not working."

"I can't," Anna said, all too quickly.

"Why's that?" her dad asked.

"I'm meeting Martin and Rebecca for a picnic tomorrow."

"Well, I'd certainly like to see the picture. It sounds very interesting and you can all go on your picnic after we've been," said her dad.

Anna felt sick inside. "I'll have to let them know!"

"Why?" said her dad, with a smile on his face.

"It won't take long and I'm sure Martin and Rebecca will love it!" I don't think so! She wanted to say.

If they both turn up in the morning with boots, ropes and torches, surely her dad would want to know what they were planning.

She had to let Martin and Rebecca know.

Her dad pinched the tip of her nose gently.

"Why don't you give them both a call?" he said, as he left the room. "I don't want to upset any plans you may already have."

Anna felt the great weight slide out of her stomach. "Thanks, dad," she called and rushed out into the hall.

"Hello!" a voice said on the other end of the phone.

"Is that you Martin?"

"If it's my number you dialled, then yes, I guess it is!" came the response.

Martin was always ready with an answer and usually not the one you expected. "A simple yes would have done," said Anna irritated.

"Look," she said, "Dad wants to take us to the museum first thing."

"Why? What have you said?"

"Just shut up Martin and listen. Susan Green has been here. She told my mum that she wanted to talk to me about the old painting in the museum. Rebecca was right. She and her friends were looking for us. And when mum told dad what had happened and that she had called, he asked me what was so important about an old painting?"

"What did you say?" Martin shouted down the phone.

"I'm not stupid! You always think that because I'm the youngest. Maybe I should go and tell dad what we've found and then they can sort it out."

"Hang on!" said Martin. "Don't you want to know what's down there?"

"Not sure I do anymore?" she replied.

"Oh come on Anna, it's not everyday you get a chance of a real adventure. The closest we ever get to excitement around here is if the cows get out onto the road or the bus is late."

"Okay, Martin, what do we do?"

"I'm not sure, I'll think of something, leave it with me."

"Are we still having a picnic?"

"No," he said, "let's get the museum out of the way first. I'll let Rebecca know. See you at ten tomorrow. Bye." The phone went dead.

"Well," said her father as she entered the sitting room. "Is he coming?"

"Yes, he's still coming over at ten tomorrow and he'll let Rebecca know."

"Where are you having your picnic?" her father said keeping his eyes fixed on the television.

"We're not having one now. Martin said we can do something else when we get back."

"Okay," came the quick response, "I want to watch this now."

Anna climbed onto the sofa next to her mum. She rested her head on her mum's lap and fell asleep.

The next morning was damp and cold. "Good job you're not having a picnic," said Anna's dad from behind the newspaper.

Anna ate her cereals and toast, got dressed and was now sitting by the window keeping an eye out for Martin and Rebecca.

When they arrived she quickly ran down the path to the gate to meet them. "Well," she said looking directly at Martin. "What's the plan now?"

"Don't panic, Anna," he said putting his arm around her shoulder. "Let's get this trip out of the way."

"How can you be sure it's going to be okay?" Anna's heart was now racing and she was sure she was going to be sick. "Once dad gets talking to Susan Green, he's bound to want to know more about the mine."

"Well!" he said, with a grin on his face. "The museum will be closed."

"Don't you remember? Susan Green said she was not working because the museum was having some changes or repairs done, or something? I can't remember, but she definitely said she would not be going to work!"

"So, if we go with your dad he'll be as surprised as we will be when we find it closed."

"That's brilliant," said Anna who wasn't sure if she should be angry or not, having had only a few restless hours sleep. "You could've let me know last night," she snarled at Martin.

"Don't worry Anna, he only reminded me that it was closed on the way over," said Rebecca.

Martin smiled apologetically at both of them. Anna's dad pulled up in the car. "Jump in," he said. Anna sat in the front and Martin and Rebecca got in the back. "Belts on," Anna's dad instructed.

It wasn't long before they were pulling into a parking space outside the museum. "Come on, let's get in and see this painting," Anna's dad was way ahead of the three of them.

"He's keen," said Martin. "Can't wait to see the look on his face, when he reaches the door."

They all froze as Anna's dad held the door open. "Come on! In you go," he said, gesturing with his free hand like he was guiding traffic.

They had only just got inside when, from nowhere, Susan Green appeared. "Well, good morning to you all," she said as she approached them with her hand out stretched to greet them.

Anna's dad stepped forward and shook Mrs Green's hand. "Clive Roberts," he said, "Anna's dad. Pleased to meet you. My wife told me you had called by with information about a painting Anna had been looking at? I'd like to see it, if that's possible?"

"Well, I'm afraid it's bad news! The paintings had to be removed from display due to an aging problem. The canvas can crack over time, so we have to take care of it, or it just gets worse."

"That's a pity," said Anna's dad looking across at the children.

"Do you want to take a look around? There's a lot to see and I'd love to give you a tour now you've come all this way."

Susan Green held her hand out showing them the way in. Mr Roberts and Susan Green walked in front of the children.

All three had only two things on their minds right now. When would they be out of here? And back into the safety of the car?

"You can see the painting has been removed. Thank goodness it wasn't one of the large ones," she said pointing to a large oil painting hanging on the opposite side of the gallery.

They moved on and after a slow procession through the many halls and levels they arrived back at the entrance.

"Well thank you so much for that," said Anna's dad, shaking Susan Green's hand. "Well, say thank you," he said looking at the three children who were now standing by the door.

"Just a moment." The children froze as Susan Green disappeared behind a kiosk door.

"There you go," she said pushing bits of card into the three children's hands. "They're free passes to our special anniversary opening.

"Invited guests only! Some very important people will be here showing off some of the new exhibitions and displays. Hope you can come and you too," Susan handed more passes to Mr Roberts.

"Thank you," he said.

"I hope to see you again soon!" Susan Green said, as she watched them leave the building.

"You've all been very quiet!" Anna's dad looked at his two passengers as he reversed onto the drive.

"Thank you very much," said Martin, who was already halfway out of the car.

Rebecca thanked Mr Roberts and stepped out of the car. "Coming in for some lunch?" he said.

"I need to let mum know I'm back," said Rebecca.

"That's okay, call from here, and you, Martin. Come on in and have something with us. I'm sure Anna will be only too pleased to have her best friends for lunch."

Having made their calls they were all sitting at the table. Mrs Roberts had placed various jars of pickles and jams on the table and the smell of freshly baked bread filled the room.

Mr Roberts was busy cutting thick slices from the loaf and handing them to each of the children.

"Come on Martin," said Mrs Roberts, "get stuck in, have whatever you want, there's plenty more."

No one felt much like eating after the shock of meeting Susan Green. They were all feeling a bit shaken and sick. "Come on, Martin, you can do better than that," said Mrs Roberts, piling even more food onto his plate.

"Thank you," Martin said, wishing he'd gone home.

Martin sat back in his chair, unable to move. He had eaten so much he felt like an over inflated ball. "Can we go upstairs?" Anna asked.

"Yes, why not. Shoes off first and no loud music. Your dad needs a rest after all this excitement today," answered Mrs Roberts.

Having removed their shoes all three ran up the stairs to the safety of Anna's bedroom.

Martin walked over to the window and scanned the street below. He sighed with relief to see the street empty.

"I half expected to see Susan and her friends sat in their car outside," said Martin.

"Oh, Martin, you're beginning to scare us all. Just sit down." Rebecca patted the bed, hoping Martin would listen to her for once.

"Look, we can't do anything today and my guess is that Susan Green isn't going to be doing much either," continued Rebecca.

"If she's at the museum working then she can't just pop off to the mine."

"I guess that's true," he said, still looking over at the window.

"So, we can meet tomorrow and hopefully get down to the wall again and see if we can find the entrance to the other tunnel," said Rebecca.

Anna looked at her two friends, "How clever they were," she thought to herself. "Are we still taking food?" she said.

"Yes," said Martin "But not a lot. Crisps, chocolate, that sort of thing."

"I think mum's got some cans of pop I can bring," said Rebecca.

"Great, let's meet at ten o'clock. We'll meet you here, Anna," said Martin.

"We should be down at the wall by eleven. That gives us at least six hours to find the other tunnel," continued Martin.

They carried on talking, deciding what each of them would bring in the morning.

Martin looked at his phone it was his mum. "Got to go," he said. He stood and walked over to the door. They all clambered down the stairs.

"Here they come. Our light footed elephants!" said Anna's dad, who was just coming out of the kitchen with a hot drink in one hand and a book in the other.

"Do you want a drink before you go?" he asked, waving his steaming cup of tea towards Martin and Rebecca.

"No thank you, we have to get home for tea."

"He means dinner," said Anna looking across at Martin, who was now turning a funny shade of red.

"Whatever!" Anna's dad returned to his chair in front of the television. "See you in the morning," Anna said as she closed the door, locking it quickly, just in case.

Hidden strength

It was a clear, sunny day as Rebecca and Martin walked along the road that lead to Anna's house.

They both nervously scanned the streets for Susan Green's car. "Come on," said Martin who was almost running.

"Okay," said Rebecca, "I have got all this to carry."

Her arms were full, holding a large rope, a bag containing her boots, as well as her torch.

Anna was sat on the steps waiting. She too had a large plastic bag and her boots slung over her shoulder. "What's that?" said Martin pointing to a very large bag.

"It's my lamp!"

"I thought we agreed to bring torches?"

"It's good," said Anna. "Honest! It's really good! Better than a torch."

"Okay," said Martin, "show us when we get there."

They all set off down the lane to the beach. It wouldn't be long before they were back at the great black wall.

Having changed into their boots and looping the ropes across their chests, all three looked like real explorers, about to set off on an expedition to some foreign country or unknown jungle.

"Let's see this lamp of yours then, Anna." Martin grabbed the bag sitting beside Anna.

He took the lamp out and switched it on. "That's good!" he said. "It doesn't even work!"

"It does!" said Anna grabbing it back. "You need to charge it first." She began frantically winding the handle on the side of the lamp.

"Now try," she passed it back to Martin.

"That's good, pity you've got to wind it though."

"I can leave it here if you don't want it!" said Anna, placing it back in the bag.

"Don't be so mean, Martin," said Rebecca. "You bring it Anna. We need as much light as possible down there and, if we want to find that passage, the more light we have the better." Anna pulled the lamp from the bag and smiled across at Rebecca.

"Come on!" called Martin as he ran towards the path leading to the entrance.

All of the branches and leaves they had placed over the path were still in place. "That's good," he said, pulling them aside to make a path to the entrance. "At least we know they haven't been here yet."

They entered the tunnel and proceeded along its length to the shaft. Martin threw his rope down. "I'll go first," said Rebecca. She had pushed her torch into her belt with the beam facing down at her feet.

"That'll help me see the floor when I reach the end of the ladder," she informed the others.

Slowly, she lowered herself into the darkness and onto the floor of the great hall.

As she landed she felt strange. She couldn't decide what it was, but there was something different. It wasn't a bad feeling but it was definitely different.

Martin had pulled the rope up and secured it around Anna's waist. "Good job you're not as big as Rebecca or I'd never have been able to lower you down there."

"I heard that!" came an echoing voice.

"You know what I mean," said Martin. Anna had reached the floor and Rebecca was removing the rope from her waist as Martin landed, with a thud, beside them both.

"That was quick!" said Anna.

"I thought so too! Said Rebecca. "That would've been great if you'd broken your ankle!"

"I know!" said Martin, who realised he had almost jumped down to the floor, having let go of the rope at least 3 metres from the ground.

"Well, I'm okay, so let's get over to the wall and start looking for that passage."

The cavern filled with the whirring sound of Anna charging her lamp. She switched it on. "Great light," said Martin, trying to make up for upsetting Anna earlier.

"I told you it would be good," she said, looking back at Martin.

As they neared the wall, the familiar sound of ringing became louder. "It's amazing, once you're this close to the wall!" Martin had cupped his ears to ensure he was picking up every note as it rang out.

The great wooden beam was rising and falling just as before, each time dropping and producing the ringing sound from the crystals.

They all began searching the cavern for the other tunnel. "Lets' spread out," said Martin. "I'll go this way. Anna you go with Rebecca, okay?"

The two girls headed to the opposite side of the cavern. "Be sure not to get too close to the edge of that drop next to the wall. I don't know how deep it is and we may never be able to get out of it," called Martin.

Anna held Rebecca's hand tightly. Slowly they searched for signs of another tunnel, moving the beam from the torch across the damp, shining walls.

"See anything?" Martin's voice echoed from the other side of the cavern.

"Nothing here!" Rebecca replied. Turning to look in the direction of the light coming from Martin's lamp. Rebecca suddenly fell. The ground had collapsed beneath her feet.

Anna's grip tightened. Having heard the scream, Martin ran over to see what was wrong. As he looked into the hole in the floor, he was amazed to see Anna holding onto the ledge with one hand, and pulling Rebecca with the other.

With very little effort Anna hauled Rebecca out of the hole until she was able to grab onto the ledge with her free hand.

Martin reached down grabbing Anna's arm. He lifted her out onto the floor of the cavern, along with Rebecca.

They all just sat on the floor looking at the hole, then back at each other. Anna began to laugh. It wasn't long before the other two joined in.

"What's happened?" said Rebecca, looking at Martin.

"I don't know?" He said. "But what I was going to say earlier, I'd got that funny feeling again, like the feeling I had when we came down here before."

"I know what you mean," said Rebecca. "Where's Anna?" They both turned to see Anna climbing to the top of a large pile of rocks, her lamp now standing on the floor, lighting the way.

"What you doing Anna?"

"Look what I can do," she called back. Before Martin and Rebecca could do anything, Anna had leapt from the top and, with one summersault, had landed on the floor alongside her lamp.

"Hang on!" said Martin "careful you don't hurt yourself! We'll be in real trouble of any of us gets injured."

"I'm fine," she said, brushing the dust from her jeans. Martin stood and began to jump in the air. First it was only a few centimetres, then as he continued he was jumping at least two metres into the air.

Anna joined in, jumping on the spot. Rebecca reluctantly climbed to her feet and half heartedly jumped. The feeling she got as her feet left the floor made her laugh out loud. She continued until she was jumping as high as the others.

"How's this happening?" she shouted.

"I don't know?" came the reply.

"It's magic," said Anna. "It's magic."

"It's something," said Martin who was feeling more amazing with each jump. "Hang on!" he said. "Everybody stop."

"We have to find the passage before we run out of time." The three of them now started searching the cavern again, this time fully focused on the task.

After an hour of searching and researching they stood in front of the great wall. "Well, I give up! We've looked everywhere," said Martin as he sat on the floor, looking very disappointed.

"Don't say that," said Anna.

"I'm sure it's here somewhere," said Rebecca, who was studying her copy of the plan.

"I don't see where it can be," said Martin. "We've been up and down these walls for more than an hour and found nothing." Anna then turned to Rebecca and whispered something in her ear.

"What are you saying, Anna?" Martin was not happy that the two girls appeared to be laughing at him. "What's so funny?" Martin had his back to the black wall and the noise from the crystals rang out giving him no chance of catching whatever it was Anna was saying to Rebecca.

He turned and glared at the wall as if it had beaten him in some way. "Anna's found it," shouted Rebecca, with a smile on her face.

"Where?"

"There!"

"Where?"

"There, above your head."

"Anna spotted it when we sat down here. The shine from the black rock face blocked it out but from down here you can see it easily," continued Rebecca.

Martin turned and looked up above his head. There it was, plain as day, a tunnel no bigger than two metres wide and two metres high. "Okay," said Martin. "How do we get up there?"

"Well, I think we have to use that beam," said Anna, pointing at the rocking beam as it began to rise once more.

"Look, every time it rocks, that end rises up to the entrance and then drops back down again."

"You are so clever," said Martin. "Without you we would never have found the way in." Anna felt so good hearing Martin say such a nice thing about her.

She no longer felt like the little girl who tagged along with the two older children. She felt as much part of this adventure as the others.

"Come on," said Martin. "I think you're right. Look at this!" He shone his torch down at the floor. "There!" he said. "Can you see it? Looks like a path that's been worn into the floor and it ends here," he said.

123

He was now standing on a large flat stone facing the wall of water. The beam stopped, momentarily, opposite the flat slab, then began to rise again.

Martin looked down into the deep dark ravine. "I hope we're right," he said, looking up at the beam as it began to lower once more. As it paused level with the stone Martin stepped forward.

The next thing he knew his foot had slipped on the wet slimy surface and he was now lying flat on his back across the beam. He couldn't move.

Every time he tried to stand he slipped further down the beam, which was now at an even steeper angle. "Hang on," the girls shouted up to him.

He lay motionless as the beam proceeded to the top of its stroke. He was now too far along the beam to reach the tunnel. The beam began to drop. "Rebecca," he called. "Get the rope and throw it to me when the beam comes down again."

"If I try to move I'll be off here and we all know where I'll end up." Anna looked down into the ravine, it looked bottomless.

Rebecca stood waiting for the right moment to throw the rope. "Now!" called Martin.

She threw the rope in his direction. "I've got it. Now, when I say, pull me onto the ledge. I hope you still have your new found strength."

Anna had joined Rebecca on the rope. "Now!" They both pulled sending Martin flying through the air, past them both. He landed with a dull thud. He was now surrounded by clouds of black dust.

He stood coughing and spluttering, trying to speak. "Well, that was close," he said eventually, wiping the dust from his eyes.

"Why don't I try," said Anna. "I'm a lot smaller than you and I'm good at balancing."

"I knew that ballet dancing would come in useful one day," said Rebecca.

"Okay," said Martin, "but I'm tying this around you first." He held up one of the ropes. "At least if you fall off we can stop you falling all the way down there."

Anna stood waiting for the beam. Martin held Rebecca by the waist and she in turn held onto Anna's hand.

"Be careful," she said as Anna moved forward to be closer to the beam.

"I will," she said and stepped forward. Her foot slipped as the other came in contact with the beam.

Rebecca still had her hand and steadied her until she stood motionless on the beam.

"Bend your knees," said Martin as the beam rose, "or you'll slide across the beam like I did then you won't be able to reach the tunnel."

Anna now crouched and felt like a tiger about to leap through a flaming hoop. "Now!" Martin called, "Jump!" Anna landed just inside the entrance.

"Come on," she said, holding the rope, "I'll pull you both up." It was amazing how easily Anna lifted them both up to the tunnel.

"You're like Super Woman," Martin said, squeezing Anna's arm. "Now let's get a move on we're running out time."

They moved along the narrow passage. "How are you feeling Martin?" asked Rebecca.

"Do you know what! I feel fantastic."

"Well, I thought you'd be hurt after landing like you did."

"So did I," said Martin running his hands over his body to see if he had any injuries. "No, I'm fine."

They had walked a long way from the tunnel entrance, Anna leading the way with her lamp held high, lighting the whole passage with a dim glow.

"What's that?" Anna said suddenly.

"Oh no," said Martin. "It looks like the passage has collapsed."

In front of them a tangle of supports and beams blocked the way forward.

Martin lifted his torch and began to inspect the beams. The first had fallen diagonally across the passage and was leaning against the support beam on the opposite side. Then on top of this lay a cross beam.

"I don't like the look of this," he said. "If we move this," he said shining his torch onto one of the cross beams blocking the passage, "I think the others will fall and the roof will come down!"

"What if we lift them together?" Anna said. "That will keep the one at the top in place."

"Do you mean the cross beam," Rebecca interrupted.

"Yes that's the one! The cross beam."

"Well, I think that's our only option without them out of the way, we can't get to the others," said Martin, cleaning some of the rocks away from around the fallen beams. "Are you sure we can do this?"

"Look at the size of the beam!" Rebecca moved her beam of light along the length of the beam overhead. "Well we have to do something, Martin."

Martin stood next to the support to the right of the tunnel. The two girls were positioned next to the support on the left. "Right, on three we push these supports back. Let's hope that cross beam stays in place."

The command echoed down the passage. "One, two, three." Suddenly the supports were back in place, holding the cross beam firmly against the roof of the tunnel.

"That was easy," said Martin, shaking his arms and flexing his muscles.

"Yes, it was," said Rebecca.

"It didn't feel heavy to me," said Anna rubbing the top of her arm, expecting to find it bulging with muscle.

"I tell you, Martin, something strange has happened to us, look at the strength we now have," said Rebecca.

"You lifted that support with very little effort and Anna and I did the same with that one."

"I don't understand how we could have done that so easily."

"Me neither," came the reply.

Anna was now looking at the other fallen beams. "I don't think the tunnels collapsed," she said holding her lamp higher. "I think it's just that the beams have fallen over."

"I don't think they fell at all," said Martin. "I think they've been pulled over. Look!" he shone his torch down the passage way. "There's nothing on the floor of the tunnel so it hasn't collapsed."

"I tell you, someone or something pulled these beams over to stop anyone else getting through to the other side," said Anna.

With their new found strength they proceeded to clear the passage, pushing the supports back into place.

Once clear of the tangle of timber they moved slowly into the darkness.

The air was much drier now as they moved further from the wall of water. And the tunnel had grown much larger. Anna was now bouncing along each stride being a good two metres.

"Not so fast," said Martin. "We don't know what's in there." Anna stood still until the others caught up. Her lamp dimmed.

"What's wrong?" asked Martin.

"Nothing! Just waiting for you to catch up."

Anna and Rebecca linked arms and followed Martin as he edged his way along the tunnel, running his hands over the walls as if he were trying to locate a join or crack.

"Can you feel that? It's warm!"

Anna and Rebecca immediately placed their hands on the wall. "It is," they both answered.

Rebecca's torch suddenly went out, making her jump. She returned to Anna's side and linked arms. "At least yours is still working," she said giving Anna a hug.

"Yes," Anna replied. "I wind it as I'm walking along to keep it charged and it seems to keep it going."

"Well, if you want me to do some winding I don't mind," said Rebecca.

"Yes, okay but I'll do it for now."

Anna didn't want to give the lamp to anyone. The glow of it made her feel safe. Not being in control of it would make her feel insecure, scared even.

"What's that?" asked Anna as she looked ahead. They moved closer. They were now standing in front of a large wooden doorway, the frame itself carved with strange symbols and images.

The frame supported two very solid doors. "These must be a metre thick," said Martin stretching his arms out as a measure.

One of the great doors was partially open. Martin shone his torch into the darkness. His beam didn't hit any other walls or beams.

It was as if he were shining the light out into the night sky. Anna bumped into Martin, trying to see inside. "Sorry," she said rubbing Martin's back. Rebecca was now pushing Anna further forward.

"Let us in, Martin," she called from behind Anna.

Martin moved forward allowing the girls to pass.

"How big is this?" Rebecca said.

"Massive," said Anna.

"I think it's bigger than that," said Martin, who was struggling to take in the view in front of him.

Danger in the dark

The cavern was much larger than the great hall. The floor was cluttered with piles of boulders, rocks and old timbers.

There was no sense of order, each pile randomly cluttering the floor. They walked between each one. Some stood at least thirty metres high.

"What are they?" Anna asked.

"I don't know," said Rebecca. "What do you think Martin?"

"Just looks like piles of wood and rocks."

"I can't see that they serve any purpose."

"But there's so many," said Rebecca.

"There's well over twenty of these piles," Martin continued.

"More than fifty," said Anna joining in the discussion.

The air hung with a strange rotting smell. "Smells like something's died down here." Martin walked over to one of the piles. "Come on," he said, "let's get up to the top of this one. We can get a better view from up there."

He swung his torch, indicating the direction to the top. They climbed steadily, single file as Martin picked a route through the rocks and jagged timbers.

Because the cavern was so large the torch and lamp lit the far wall with only a dim glow.

They could not see the eyes looking back at them. They stood in silence, each trying to work out what the piles meant and why they were here.

The silence was broken by a very strange sound. It was a blood curdling howl. It reminded Martin of the call wolves make, howling at the moon.

No one said anything. Rebecca felt Anna's hand tighten. "Don't be scared," she said. "I'm sure it's nothing." Her comments did nothing to comfort Anna as her voice was broken by the trembling nerves in her body.

"Quiet, you two, whatever it is knows we are here." Another noise came from the other side of the cavern causing Martin to turn and face the direction from where the sound came.

As he turned, the torch's beam passed over a long black body lying flat on the floor. Trying hard not to show the girls how scared he now was, Martin steadied his hands.

Whatever it was remained motionless. "Is it Dead?" Anna whispered. No reply came from Martin, he was too scared to say anything.

"Get down," he said. They crouched beside a large bolder. Martin stood up and shone the beam back to the spot where the thing lay. "It's gone," he said. "Quick, turn your lamp out Anna."

It was now dark and very lonely. Martin's mind raced as he tried to figure out what to do next. All they had to defend themselves with was a couple of lengths of rope, two torches and a lamp.

The noise of something moving on the floor got louder. Then it became clear that whatever it was, was now climbing the pile they were on. Anna started to cry. "Quiet, Anna please! It will find us soon enough!"

In desperation Rebecca placed her hand over Anna's mouth. "Shush," she said in her ear.

They could now hear the thing breathing, louder and louder as it moved closer.

Martin stood up. "Come on!" he said, "you don't scare me." He waved his torch beam as if it were some kind of sabre.

The black shape froze once more. Martin lowered his torch. The creature stirred again. Martin quickly shone his torch back in the direction of the sound. The shape dropped and froze as before.

"I think it doesn't like the light," said Anna between tears.

"I think you're right," said Martin. He moved the beam of light away, once more, then quickly swung it back. The thing was caught in the beam before it had chance to lie back down. It stood on four legs and was jet black. It was at least two metres to its front shoulders.

Martin repeatedly swung the torch away and then back again. Each time the creature moved closer. "Anna give me your lamp." He turned it on and held it high above his head.

The black shape dropped to the floor. "I think it's the light?" He shouted as he climbed on top of the large rock they had been hiding behind.

"Come up here, Anna. Hold this up here." He swung the lamp then passed it to Anna who took his place on top of the rock.

Martin climbed down and walked towards the black shape spread flat on the floor. As he got nearer, whatever it was started to crawl backwards away from him.

Martin made sure the beam stayed on the creature. "Yes!" he yelled "back you go. Look it's backing away, it doesn't like the light."

Martin moved forward once more. Again the black shape moved away from his beam. "See," he said. He could see Anna standing on top of the rock. He was at least 10 metres from her.

The words "Come and join me" had just left his mouth when the light in his hand faded. He could no longer see what lay in front of him, but he could hear clearly the sound of claws scrapping the rocks on the floor of the cavern.

He didn't wait to see how close the creature was before starting to run back to the rock where Anna was now screaming at him.

"Come on Martin! You can do it, don't stop!" Rebecca was also calling out instructions, urging him not to stop. He reached the base of the rock and in one leap he landed beside Anna.

The creature cowered below, snarling. It sniffed the air and lifted its head. All at once the cavern filled with the sound of howling. It was coming from everywhere.

"How many are there?" said Rebecca.

"I don't know," said Martin, "but we can't stay here. Anna you make sure you keep that lamp of yours going. It's the only thing between us and whatever it is out there."

Anna did not need asking twice. She began winding the handle as fast as she could. The more she wound the handle the brighter the lamp glowed. "Well done Anna," Rebecca whispered in her ear.

Martin was now looking in all directions. "What is it Martin?" Rebecca asked, her voice now trembling.

"Where's the rope you had?"

"Down there!" Rebecca pointed behind them.

"I took mine off to climb up here with Anna," said Rebecca. "And I took mine off because you'd taken yours off," said Anna.

"Do you always do what Rebecca does?" Martin snapped.

"No, but I do if you do it," shouted Anna.

Martin felt stupid. Anna had only removed her rope because that's exactly what he had done to climb the rock quicker.

"We've got to get them," he said. "Come on, bring your lamp, Anna. If you hold it high it should be enough light to keep them away long enough so I can retrieve the ropes."

Slowly they retraced there steps to the other end of the rock. "There they are!" said Anna pointing down to the two ropes on the floor.

"I'll get them," said Martin. "You just make sure you keep that lamp lit for all our sakes." Every time Martin advanced, the sound of snarling and scraping of claws drew nearer to him. He was sure the smell of rotting meat had become stronger.

Martin reached down for the ropes and was threading them onto his arm as one of the creatures made a lunge for his hand.

It was there, in the dim light, that Martin got a good view of his black pursuer. He pulled his hand back quickly and fell against the base of the rock. Slowly he climbed up the steep incline.

This was made harder because he was now somehow walking on hands and feet looking up at the roof of the cavern, like some sort of giant crab.

Too scared to take his eyes off the floor below him, he continued to crawl up higher until he reached Anna and Rebecca and the relative safety of the lamp.

"That was too close," he said. "It almost had me and I'm sure it would have dragged me off into the darkness and that would have been the end of...."

He stopped mid sentence. "But it didn't and I am still in one piece."

"We can't stay up here. I think we should go back," Anna's voice was trembling with fear. She wanted an adventure, not this!

"Yes, I agree," said Martin. "Whatever it is that Susan Green wants down here, she can have it."

"Before we start back lets tie ourselves together. That way we can be sure we stay as close to the lamp as possible. Those things won't come anywhere near it for some reason," he said.

Martin threw the rope around Rebecca's waist and secured it firmly. "You next," he said, pulling Anna closer to Rebecca.

You can hold your lamp in the middle then we can all be given some protection. He finally finished tying the rope around himself.

Once down off the rock, they walked in step to avoid kicking each other. This would be no time to stumble and drop the lamp.

They were making good progress, even though the cavern was still filled with howling and snarling. "Just focus on reaching that door," he yelled at the girls. "Don't look back just keep following me."

He led on. "Not far now!" he said "we'll soon be on the other side of that door."

From nowhere, a blinding light appeared and an all too familiar voice echoed all around them.

"So there you are! Look at the three of you! Guess you think you are very clever? Well you will soon find out where your little adventure has got you."

"I'm amazed they're still alive," Mr Richardson said, shining his very bright flood light into the children's eyes.

"My dad knows we are here," said Anna with panic in her voice.

"Does he now?" Susan Green knelt down on one knee and gripped Anna's chin in her hand. "Funny you should say that because he seems to think you have all gone for a nice picnic?"

She laughed out loud then stood up. "What do we do with you now? I guess we can leave you to my special friends."

"You have already met the dogs," she said, waving a hand in the direction of the cavern.

"You see, I can't risk taking you back out. Who knows what you might tell them."

"We've got nothing to tell them," said Martin.

"Oh I am sure that's what you'll say now! But once you've had time to think about everything I am sure you'll have to tell someone. If you can find someone who will believe you that is?"

"I promise we won't tell them anything. All we have seen is the black water and some old broken furniture. Who's going to be interested in that?" said Rebecca.

"What about this?"

Susan reached down and lifted a very large bolder from the floor. She threw it and it disappeared into the darkness and then crashed against a far wall.

"That's what I mean! Haven't you noticed how much stronger you are?"

Martin squeezed the girl's hands. That was enough for them to understand that he wasn't about to say anything. All three remained silent.

"How about you?" Susan tugged on the rope around Martin's waist.

"Well," she said, "lost your tongue?"

Martin stood and looked at Susan. "If you let us go we will show you what we have found."

"Why?" snapped Susan. Her eyes were full of anger. "What have you found?" Martin's heart was beating hard.

Susan released the rope and turned to her companions.

They were talking just loud enough for Martin to hear. "Well we can't let them out of here they know too much."

Martin lowered his voice and whispered to Anna and Rebecca.

"Look we can't just stand here like dummies. This could be our only chance. Just do as I say." Martin now had his arms wrapped around each of them.

As Susan turned to face them her lamp shone in their eyes. All they could see was the dark silhouette of Susan green behind the bright light.

"Jump!" shouted Martin. The three of them left the floor and landed with a crash.

They crouched on top of the large boulder, hidden by a cloud of thick black dust.

Susan Green's torch scanned the darkness passing over their heads.

"Keep down," whispered Martin. His arms over Rebecca and Anna's heads for protection.

"Come on down! We don't want to have to come up there!" The words made Martin shudder.

"Look, we can all be out of here in no time. We know a quick way back to the top don't we Clive."

Martin could just about make out the shape of three people standing below.

"They must think we are stupid," Martin whispered under his breath.

He could hear Rebecca and Anna breathing heavily, breathless with fear.

"Don't worry," he said, reassuringly. It was very quiet and the beam of light, that had been moving all over the cavern, was now still.

The silence was suddenly broken by Susan's voice. She was now shouting.

"You don't get it, do you?" She called out to them. "You just did something that was quite amazing, don't you think Clive?"

Susan looked across at Mr Richardson. He looked back with a confused look on his face. She continued, "you just managed to jump, what do you reckon Clive? Twenty metres, maybe more, in one go!"

"I'd say that was pretty good considering! How do you think that happened? Maybe you have developed wings or some sort of magical power?"

"Well, let me let you in to a little secret! It's nothing!" Anna and Rebecca had both now lifted their heads from under Martin's protective arms.

"I've told you about this strange substance that exists down here. I guess you haven't found a seam yet. But! I can assure you it's everywhere. It's in the very air you're breathing."

"Look," she said shining her lamp around the walls of the great cavern.

"Each one of these tunnels was being mined for one thing and one thing only, nothing! Everyone wanted nothing!"

"Because of its powers that increase any ones strength and its ability to cure almost any sickness, everybody wanted it."

"The problem with nothing however, was that it became addictive."

"Everyone became so addicted that they couldn't live without it."

"The more you had the more you wanted. The thing with nothing is, that over time, if you breathe it in long enough it starts to take effect on your body."

"As you have discovered with our not so little friends."

She shone her torch in the direction of the large dogs who were still cowering on the floor.

"They were just small puppies when we brought them down here. But, as you can see, because they have been trapped down here for years, they have now grown into the giants they are today."

"They have survived because they have developed the ability to live in complete darkness."

"I guess that's why they drop to the floor whenever a torch beam hits them."

Recalling their own earlier experiences it all made sense to Martin and the girls. "There is something else about nothing, if you haven't already worked it out," continued Miss Green.

"If you expose it to light the effects are instant. That's why you could jump so far. It must have been my light that gave you your strength. So I guess you're beginning to feel much weaker up there on your little rock fortress."

"Well, I'm sure you won't last long. Your torches will run out of power and the dogs will do the rest."

"Come on," she turned her lamp on PC Golding and Mr Richardson. "Let's get out of here."

Martin and the girls watched as the light faded as the great wooden doors slammed shut.

"Quick," he said. "Get that lamp going, Anna. It's our only protection and I need time to think."

The whirl of the lamp being charged echoed around them as the light grew brighter.

The sound of the dogs moving closer stopped once the lamp burst into life.

"Keep it going, Anna," called Martin, now scanning the darkness trying to locate the dogs as they hid from the light.

Trapped

They could hear the sound of voices clearly. "They're still out there," cried Anna.

"Amazing how well we can hear them through that solid door," said Rebecca.

Martin turned to her. "Nothing is truly magical. It not only increases your physical strength but must also increase the power of all our senses."

"That's why the smell of rotten flesh became greater and why we can hear them talking so clearly."

They all looked down at the closed door. "I don't like this place," said Rebecca. "Me neither," said Anna.

"They won't be getting out of there in a hurry!" It was Susan Green's voice.

The talking continued. "I told you this was all going to go wrong from the start."

"They're only kids! You said," yelled Susan Green.

"Who's going to believe them! You said." She continued.

"Shut up, Susan," said Mr Richardson. "Look they're trapped in there and that's where they will stay. There is no way out!"

"We'll just seal this door by letting the tunnel collapse."

The sound of hammering rang out. "Come on, a few more blows and she'll fall," said Susan.

"What are they doing?" Rebecca shouted above the noise, looking across at Martin.

"I think they're trying to knock the roof supports out." Anna began to sob.

"Don't cry! I'll get us out I promise!" Martin squeezed Anna's hand gently.

Anna pulled it away. "You said that when we first came in."

Martin felt bad enough that he's got his best friends involved in this terrible mess.

"I'm your friend to the end," he said, "and I will get you both out of here."

"It's gone quiet," said Rebecca. The sound of hammering stopped.

"Have they gone?" Anna was now wishing she was home watching TV with her mum.

The sound of Susan's voice returned. "Come on, Clive. Let's get this over with."

"Just one more smash and she's down," he replied.

"You're right. Get on with it so we can get out of here." It was PC Golding's voice.

"Wondered when he was going to join in," Martin said through gritted teeth.

Suddenly, there was a loud bang as the hammer hit the support again. This was followed by the sound of timbers cracking.

"Get out of here," was the last thing they heard before the sound of timber breaking and rocks falling filled the air.

The dust rose in large black clouds covering everything including the children who had huddled together for protection.

It was now silent and Anna's little lamp struggled to pierce the darkness. As the dust settled the particles sparkled as they floated to the floor.

Escape

The entrance was now blocked and they all knew it was the only way out.

Martin scanned the cavern. "I don't think there's any other way out of here."

Anna began to cry, she wanted to be back outside breathing the fresh sea air and running on the beach. "No one knows we are here!" she said in between tears.

Rebecca put her arm around Anna's shoulders. "Come on, we'll be fine," trying to convince herself as much as Anna.

"Time to start thinking!" said Martin. "Come on Anna. Where's that wonderful brain of yours when we need it?" they sat huddled together.

Anna's lamp lit the cavern. Their eyes became more accustomed to the dim glow.

They were surrounded by piles of rock and rubble, old twisted metal frames and pulleys. Anna then caught sight of a steel cable passing through the length of the cavern. It still had some pulleys on it.

"Look!" she said to the others. "I don't know what's blocking the exit and I don't think we can lift those rocks, even with our new found strength."

She pointed to the large boulders stacked in front of the door. "That's obvious," said Martin. "We'd need to blast them out of the way, and, unless you've got a pocket of explosives that's never going to happen!"

"Yes," said Anna, "you're right." She looked down at the floor feeling even more hopeless than she had ever before. "Go on Anna," encouraged Rebecca. "What were you going to say?"

"Well! Look," she said, "this steel cable runs from down there." She pointed a finger at the large wooden door, "and all the way up to the top of this cavern. And do you see the pulleys on the cable?" Anna held the lamp higher to throw more light on the cable above their heads. "Maybe we can use them?"

"How?" said Martin with great interest.

"Well, the pulleys alone won't be any use. But they might if we can use them somehow?"

She placed her hand on the end of one of the beams scattered over the floor.

"How?" said Rebecca.

"Like a battering ram. One won't be enough, but ten could do some damage. I've seen pictures of battering rams used by Roman soldiers to knock down thick walls, so I think it may work."

"No!" said Martin. The girls turned and looked at him.

"You got a better idea?" asked Anna.

"No, I was going to say we only get one chance at this. If it doesn't break through, the passage will be blocked with even more obstacles."

"We should use as many as we can," said Anna.

"You're amazing," said Martin, rubbing the top of Anna's head.

Anna felt so much better. She loved it when the others treated her as an adult and not a little girl.

"Before we start, we need to think this through. Look we need to launch this ram somehow. Once we've got the beams together they're going to be very heavy." Martin's head was now full of ideas and he began to pile rocks on top of each other to form a rough pillar. "Don't just stand there watching me," he said. "All we have is the wind up lamp thing of Anna's to protect us from those hungry dogs."

"Better than nothing," she said looking down at her shiny princess lantern, she'd had as a present from her mum. "Come in handy one day," she'd said when Anna looked disappointed. How right her mum had been!

The girls were now watching Martin running around collecting large flat stones and balancing each one on top of the other.

"There," he said as he finished stacking stones to form the first pillar. "We need four of these," he continued, and showed the girls where he wanted the other pillars to be. Like a foreman on a building site he assessed the progress being made.

"Okay," he said. "We just need to place this in the middle of your pillar." Martin held up a length of timber. Carefully he laid it across the pillar that Anna had been building. "I think it needs to be a little higher," he said.

Anna lifted yet more flat rocks onto the pillar. "Great," said Martin. "Now help me find another beam about the same size as this." He was holding one of the shorter beams across his arms. "I'll need your help. It's too heavy for me on my own."

They all realised that the amazing strength that they had earlier had gone. They all lifted the first beam on top of the far pillars. "I've found one," said Anna.

Luckily it wasn't far from the pillars they had built. They lifted the second beam in place.

"Now the hard bit," said Martin. "Lucky for us the beams are close enough for us to get them on to here," he said tapping one of the smaller beams they had placed on top of the pillars.

If they all worked together they could just about lift one end of the large beams. After an hour they had finally managed to stack twenty of the beams on top of the pillars.

"That's enough," said Martin, exhausted from working so hard to get the beams in place.

"Now let's get these attached." Martin held up one of the steel cables. It was as thick as three fingers and very stiff.

After several attempts to tie the cable around the beams Martin sank to his knees.

"You can't tie this stuff, it's too hard!" he said looking down at the cable lying on the floor.

"All that work for NOTHING!"

The very word reminded them why they were here, and how much they wished they had never heard it.

"Just a minute," said Anna. She disappeared into the darkness. "Be careful," Rebecca called as she watched her friend vanish from view.

When she returned she was holding two very large spanners. "Where did you find them?" asked Martin.

"I saw them when I was looking for a way out," answered Anna.

"This may be it," Martin said, grabbing the spanners from Anna's hand.

"Hey! What do you say?" called Anna.

"Oh thank you," said Martin.

"That's better," said Anna.

Martin worked frantically to undo the cable clamps attached to the old steel cables.

Two would be sufficient he had told the girls who both sat watching him.

"Can we help?" said Rebecca.

"In a minute," came the reply. "Can you bring that clockwork lamp of yours a bit closer, Anna?"

Anna jumped to her feet and was soon at his side with Rebecca not far behind. "I'm not sitting over there on my own in the dark," she said.

Having now positioned herself she could see what Martin was doing. He managed to get two lengths of steel cable under the great wooden beams, one at the front, and one at the back.

"There, that should hold them up long enough," he said out loud.

"Come on, you two. I need your help. I need to pull the two pulleys back above this lot and then pass the steel cable through each."

"Anna, can you shine the lamp up here so that I can see the pulley wheel." Rebecca held the pulley in place above the wooden beam, whilst Martin struggled to get the cable through the pulley block. "It's hard to do this!" he said. "The cables are not only stiff but it's heavy.

There!" he said jumping down next to Anna. "Great job," he said, patting her on the head.

"Now let's get the next one threaded." Once again Rebecca held the pulley block in place. Martin jumped down off the beams and bent down with his hand on his knees.

"Wow, I need to get my breath back," he said, wiping his forehead with his now very dirty hands.

Anna began to laugh.

"What's so funny?"

"You!" said Anna. "Your face is covered, it will take a month of washing to get that lot off."

"I don't care if it takes a year, as long as this works," he said, looking up at the pulleys.

The light began to dim so the familiar sound of Anna cranking the dynamo returned.

"Brilliant thing that lamp of yours," said Martin as the light returned.

"I just need to get these clamps on and I think we will be ready to try Anna's battering ram."

A cold chill ran through them all as the sound of the dogs howling filled the air once more.

"We need to get this done before they get too close and become used to the light from your lamp," Martin looked across at Anna who was now winding harder than ever. "Don't worry," he said reaching out and rubbing her shoulder. "Let's get this finished."

Getting the clamps on was harder than Martin had anticipated and an hour later he was still trying to get the first one in place.

"It's no good," he said, sitting on the floor exhausted. "I don't think I can do it," he said.

"We can!" said Anna.

"Look, Anna, I know you want to get out of here and so do I! The problem is I can't get the clamps over the cables," said Martin looking very fed up.

"No!" Anna said. "I meant, we can! We! Not you or me or Rebecca, WE!"

"Shut up, Martin," said Rebecca who now had her arm around Anna's shoulders. "Let Anna explain."

"Look!" Anna said pointing to the steel cables. "You've only gone under the beams once, and you're now trying to hold the ends together then secure the clamps."

"Yes," Martin responded.

"Well! Why not go under the beams again and then let the cables lay side by side, across the top of the beams. Then if I stand this side and Rebecca stands on the other, we can each pull the cable in opposite directions until you get the clamps on."

"You're brilliant!" said Martin.

He'd been trying for over an hour to hold the ends of the cables together, but the weight and stiffness would not let him get the clamp over the two cables.

Anna pulled the cable with all the strength she could draw up from her tiny little frame. Rebecca had a firm grip of the other end and was pulling as hard as she could.

Martin quickly placed the clamp over the cables and tightened the nut and bolt. "That should hold," he said. "Now let's get that other clamp connected." It took a lot of effort passing the cables under and over the beams but they had done it. Both clamps were now in place and they all stood back admiring their success. "Well, we'll soon know if all this effort was worth it."

The noise of Anna winding the lamp returned once more, lighting the cavern. Martin had told the girls to move away from the path of the cable. "Just hope it's strong enough to take the weight of all these beams," he said as he walked towards the timber protruding from the pillar Anna had built.

"Hope you got this right," he said looking over at Anna. "Just get on with it Martin!" came the response from both girls.

Martin began to pull on the timber but it was going nowhere. "Guess I need a WE!" he said. The girls began to laugh. "Come on you two, get over here and give me a hand. Make sure you move clear of the beams once they start to move." As they all pushed it looked like Martin's plan would fail. Suddenly, there was a creak from the cables as the pillar collapsed, throwing up a black cloud of dust.

The noise was deafening as the other three pillars fell over. Nothing could be seen as a great cloud of black dust engulfed them all. The noise of the wheels turning on the cable grew louder and louder as the load gathered speed.

The sound of splintering wood and rattling cables was now echoing around the great cavern.

Anna began to cry and Rebecca hugged her tight. Martin threw his arms around both girls who were huddled on the floor.

Their lungs were burning and eyes stinging from so much dust. The noise continued for a while bouncing around the walls, then all was quiet. "Turn your lamp on Anna." She began winding. The dim glow from the lamp illuminated the dust now hanging in the air. They stumbled over the rubble and old beams that were scattered on the floor. "Careful!" said Martin. "There may be broken pieces and we don't want to go sticking them in our legs." The three of them made their way slowly back down the cavern, gripping hands as if their lives depended on it.

It wasn't long before they were standing in front of a pile of broken beams and rocks. Anna moved the lamp in search of a way out. At first it looked as though the battering ram had failed. Suddenly, Rebecca shouted "Look!" she said. "There! Hold the lamp up Anna, hold it up," she demanded. Anna raised the lamp and there between the roof of the cavern and the pile of broken beams and rock was a hole.

It would be big enough for them to get out. Martin suggested that he should go first to make sure it was safe. "Okay," said Rebecca. "I'll stay here at the bottom with Anna."

He made his way carefully to the top of the pile and stuck his head through the hole. "Yahoo!" he shouted, sending echoes around the cavern again.

"I'll come back down and help you two up and then we can get out of here!"

Rebecca went first. Martin holding her hand for support, she climbed the pile of rubble and wood. As she reached the hole at the top, she took one last look back at the others then, fell through the hole out of sight. "You okay?" called Martin.

"Yes fine," came the response. I'm Okay but it's very dark."

"We won't be long," said Martin as he helped Anna to the top and through the hole.

As he helped the girls climb to the hole and freedom, Martin had been watching for the dogs.

Holding the lamp up high above his head, he could see the outline of at least three.

There may have been more but he could only see three. The lamp began to dim. Martin immediately began winding the charger. The lamps glow increased as he continued to wind and whirl, it echoed around the cavern once more.

Now the lamp was charged Martin took one final look down at the floor of the cavern, then fell through the hole into the passage the other side.

As he fell he lost his grip on the lamp and it flew out of his hand. The girls watched in fear as Martin screamed with pain. Anna rushed to get the lamp. She picked it up and held it high, lighting the passage once more. Martin sat rubbing his knee. Blood ran down his shin. "It's nothing," he said.

Wiping the blood away with dirty hands, Anna and Rebecca wrapped their arms around him and helped him to stand.

"Get off!" he said. "Really, I'm okay." The girls stood back to allow Martin to stand on his own.

"Quick, Martin," Anna said as she raised the lamp. "The dogs are behind you!"

A snarling head was now clearly visible above the three of them. The creature had managed to get its head through the hole but it wasn't big enough to allow its shoulders through. The image of the dog snarling and growling caused Rebecca to scream. Martin picked up one of the rocks and threw it, striking the dog on its nose. The dog withdrew its head out of sight.

"Come on!" said Martin. "If we get back to the water wall we will be safe or at least away from the dogs."

As they ran down the tunnel there was no sign of Susan, PC Golding or Mr Richardson.

Once again, Martin and the girls lashed themselves together, as they negotiated the rocking beam that would enable them to drop down onto the floor of the great hall.

As they all stood getting their breath back, the sound of the dogs' howling filled the hall. It was clear there was more than three making so much noise.

"We're okay," said Martin looking at each of the girls.

"We've still got to climb the shaft and get out of the tunnel. Let's hope they haven't blocked it off yet!" said Rebecca.

Home

They ran to the bottom of the shaft and looked up. "Oh no," said Anna. Susan Green and her colleagues were standing around the rim at the top.

The beams from their torches held the three of them for a moment. Martin pulled the girls back out of the shaft.

"Come on, Clive, give me a hand!" Susan Green was not pleased to see the children again. She threw the other end of the rope to Clive Richardson who then lowered her down towards the children.

He and PC Golding followed her using the same rope, now secured at the top. Once down on the floor of the great hall, they all shone their torches over the expanse of broken tables and chairs.

"They must be in here somewhere," Susan Green yelled.

Her angry voice bounced around the walls of the great hall.

Martin and the girls hid under a broken table. Thank god its dark, thought Martin, lying motionless.

"Come on, we have to find them. If they get out of here they are sure to tell someone and then all this will be gone," shouted Miss Green.

The great hall fell silent except for the faint sound of dogs howling.

This sent a shiver through Rebecca. She reached out for Anna's hand and squeezed it. "Don't worry," said Anna. "Martin will think of something."

"Shush!" Martin placed a hand over Anna's mouth. She bit it hard.

Martin pulled his hand away and found it very hard not to shout out. He placed his hand under his arm to try and deaden the pain.

As long as they stayed still they would be impossible to find, amongst all of the broken furniture.

Susan's voice boomed once more. "Come on, let's get out of here."

"Look! You can't stay down here forever. You'll have to come out eventually."

The sound of them searching for the children grew louder and soon Susan and the others were stood only a few metres from where Martin, Anna and Rebecca lay.

The footsteps passed and faded into the distance. "I think they've passed," Martin said in a whispered voice. "Give it a few minutes and I'll take a look to see how far they've gone."

The sound of Susan's voice sounded again. "Come on! This is your last chance or we will leave you down here to rot." It fell silent again.

"Come on, let's get out of here!" Whispered Martin.

All three ran to the bottom of the rope hanging down the shaft.

"You go first Rebecca." She grabbed the rope and began to climb.

"Hurry! Called Martin and Anna, both eager to get away from the bottom of the shaft as there was nowhere to hide.

Rebecca reached the top and called down to let the others know.

"It's hard to see what you're doing without any light," she informed the others.

"Give me your lamp, Anna." She passed it to Martin. "Now let me tie you on. "Okay," called Martin. The rope tightened as Rebecca began to pull Anna up into the darkness of the shaft.

"Don't forget to throw the rope back down once you're on the top," called Martin.

Anna looked down at Martin, his dirty face illuminated by the lamp. "I'm sure we won't," she called back.

"Hurry then," said Martin. "I'm sure I can see them coming back!"

The torch beams appeared to be approaching Martin much faster than before.

Martin couldn't understand why at first. Then he heard the sound he dreaded.

It was the sound of dogs howling and barking and it was gradually getting louder and louder.

"Come on," he called, "they'll be here soon and they're not alone!"

Rebecca recognised panic in Martin's voice as she worked even harder to pull Anna to safety. With the dim light coming from the lamp at the bottom of the shaft, Rebecca could only see a shadow hanging onto the rope.

She reached down and felt Anna's hand close around hers.

"Come on," she said and pulled Anna onto the rim of the shaft.

Eagerly they undid the rope tied around Anna's waist. Anna grabbed the loose end and threw it out into the darkness.

It had no sooner landed than Martin grabbed it and began to climb.

He had only climbed two or three metres, when he felt a tug on the rope.

A beam of light shot over his shoulder and lit the faces of Rebecca and Anna.

"They're behind you, Martin, hurry!" He was now halfway to the top and was beginning to tire.

PC Golding had now grabbed the rope and was following him at a much faster pace than Martin could manage.

It was clear that Golding would reach him before he got to the top. Anna and Rebecca looked down helplessly at Martin.

"Come on, Martin, you can do it." They were both surprised with Martin's response.

"Untie the rope," he called.

"But you'll fall," replied Rebecca.

"Please, just do it! Untie the rope or they'll get to you and Anna!"

"We can't let you drop down there!" Floods of tears ran from Anna's eyes. Even Martin knew she was crying as the tears were dripping onto his face.

"Untie the rope, please!"

"We can't!"

"Just do it!" he pleaded.

Suddenly, Rebecca jumped to her feet and followed the rope to where it had been secured.

It took some effort but eventually she managed to get the first loop unthreaded.

She tugged at the second. With all her strength she pulled at the knotted rope.

"Do it!" Martin called. "PC Golding is less than a metre away."

Suddenly the sound of air rushing exploded as the rope fell down into the great hall.

With a dull thud PC Golding's body landed on top of Susan Green and Mr Richardson, knocking them off their feet.

The sound of the dogs erupted. The shaft was completely dark as Rebecca and Anna looked over the edge.

Both girls cried uncontrollably at the thought of Martin, lying alone at the bottom.

"Come on!" Martin's voice came from nowhere.

He was now standing behind them. The girl's tears of sadness turned to tears of joy, as Martin turned on the lamp. There he was!

"How'd you do that?" Rebecca asked.

"That stairway we found when we first came here."

"I'd almost reached it when PC Golding had started to climb the rope. It made it hard to swing over to the opening with Golding hanging onto the bottom, but I managed to reach it before he could get to me."

They all shuddered as the sound of dogs howling and barking grew louder and louder. "I guess their lamps went out," said Martin.

There was no light coming up the shaft and the howling had been replaced with the sound of dogs hungrily eating, fighting over each mouthful, tugging and tearing to get a share of the food now available.

Martin moved towards the rim of the shaft with the lamp held out in front of him.

Rebecca grabbed his arm and pulled him back. "I don't think we want to see what's down there," she said.

Martin swung around and looked at them both. "Come on, then, let's get out of here." They quickly followed the now familiar passage that led to the exit and daylight.

Unfinished business

The sun was on the horizon, getting ready to set. Never before had the sky appeared so blue and so clear.

Their eyes hurt after adjusting to the dim glow of Anna's lamp. The air smelt so fresh and the sun so warm.

Anna began to pull the broken branches and shrubs across the path to the mine. Martin and Rebecca had continued walking without her.

"Hey! What about the path," she called after them.

"Don't bother with that," said Martin. "Let someone else find it and they can sort it out."

They all met at Anna's the next day, as arranged the night before. Each one now talking about their return home and the questions they'd been asked and what they had done once the inquests had finished.

Martin sat on the steps between Anna and Rebecca.

"I've got something to show you!" Martin reached into his pocket and pulled out a small, rusty tin.

"I didn't show you yesterday because I'd forgotten about it."

"What is it?" asked Anna.

"I don't know," came the reply.

"Where's it from?" asked Rebecca, leaning closer to Martin to get a better look.

"I picked it up when we were building the stone pillars."

"Have you opened it?" interrupted Anna, now eager to see what was inside.

"No, not yet."

Slowly, Martin twisted the lid. "It's tight," he said, gripping the lid even harder. Suddenly it moved. "That's freed it," he said looking down at the tin on his lap. He twisted the lid slowly then lifted it clear.

They all covered their eyes as a bright glow came from within.

The colours were so bright, so beautiful, and so wonderful.

A strange feeling passed through them all.

It was as if someone had placed a very warm fire in front of them, then taken it away suddenly. Whatever it was left them all feeling amazing.

"Did you feel that?" said Martin looking across at Rebecca.

The two girls said nothing, they just sat smiling looking at the glow still coming from the tin.

Gradually, it faded and then it was gone.

The tin was empty.

"So, that was what it was all about! NOTHING!" Martin said, his throat now dry from shock.

"Yes," said Anna, "Nothing."

"Do you think that's the last of it?" said Rebecca.

"I don't know and I'm in no hurry to find out. Let someone else go look. I'm sure the dogs won't turn down another free meal!"

Printed in Great Britain
by Amazon